Tar Baby 2

Tammy Campbell Brooks
Tahirah Jessalyn Brooks

Tar Baby 2

Author: Tammy Campbell Brooks
Tahirah Jessalyn Brooks
Title: Tar Baby 2
Subject: fiction
American
Publishing 2019
Paradeyez Books
ISBN-13:
978-1732276840
Library of Congress Control Number: 2019939514

Table of Contents

Contents

Tar Baby 2

Please be sure to read "Tar Baby,"the predecessor of Tar Baby 2.

"Wow! I must say what a story with a jaw-dropping climax of an ending! Without giving too many spoilers, I enjoy the overall message of Tar Baby, reminding African American women that black is beautiful, regardless of the shade: light brown, brown, chocolate, dark, etc. Tar Baby is a friendly reminder that African American women's true beauty comes from within, to feel confident and fearless in your skin, and most importantly "your melanin is poppin"! The ending of Tar Baby is breathtaking. It truly leaves you anxious to see what happens next; there are so many questions! Tammy never disappoints. I'm ready for Tar Baby 2!"~ Roosevelt Broome, founder of Rich Apparel

"What! Why would you leave us hanging? Not happy book was just getting good. Good story line. I do hope the New book picks up where it left off at." ~ Amazon reviewer.

"Tammy, I really, really enjoyed this but I'm on pins and needles wondering what's going to happen in Tar Baby 2! What a cliffhanger ending!" ~Emily Hainsworth, author of Through To You.

"Ohhhh, I need answers!!! Where is part 2???"~ Monica Anthony Gantt.

"Tammy, thumbs up on Tar Baby. Finished reading last night. Mad don't want to wait until 2019, so tell me the ending. Lol." ~Mary Dayson.

"Another one of my clients read Tar Baby. She called me excited! Loved it! Can't wait until June." ~Ms.Evelyn.

Tar Baby 2

Tianna's Story

Introduction

Tianna lay unconscious on the ambulance stretcher gasping for air. She choked on her own blood as they rushed her to the hospital.

Tasha followed the ambulance in a panic. After Jackson took off in the rental car, she found the keys to Tianna's Toyota Camry.
She drove while calling Tianna's mother to tell her about the attack on her by her ex-boyfriend, Mark White. Bernadette wailed after hearing what happened to her daughter. Tasha cried with her as Bernadette made her way to Boston.

Tasha called her parents and then tried calling her brother Jackson, but he wasn't picking up. Tasha drove faster, running red lights and going way past the speed limit in hot pursuit of the ambulance on its way to the nearest hospital.

She prayed for her best friend as the ambulance pulled into the Massachusetts General Hospital emergency entrance. The first EMT, Jacob, opened the back door of the ambulance and got out. He and his partner, Rob, grabbed the stretcher to ease Tianna down and take her to emergency surgery.

The Massachusetts police department waited for Tasha to get out her car to question her on the incident. She told the officer, John, that Tianna's ex-boyfriend Mark locked her in her bedroom and began beating her. She tried to help, but the door was locked. She could hear her friend crying and begging him to stop and then she could no longer hear her cries. She kept hearing furniture smashing and that's when Mark walked out of the room carrying a knife.

Tasha began to cry more thinking of how she couldn't help Tianna. Her clothes reeked of Tianna's blood; she was distraught. She began to sob louder after seeing Tianna's chest being pumped. She heard the nurse say that they were losing her and to get a doctor STAT!

Tar Baby 2

The Tar Baby series is dedicated to all the beautiful dark-skinned sisters.

To **A**lways **R**emember you are **B**lack **A**nd **B**eautiful the way **Y**ou are.

Chapter One

Tianna sat in the crowd listening to her roommate Malcolm

speak. Her other roommate, Michelle, and four-year-old Tyler sat next to
her. It was a cold February night in Massachusetts. Snow was expected
but hadn't quite made its appearance. A cold puff of condensation could
be seen coming from Malcolm's mouth when he spoke.

"We must unite or die! It is the only way we'll ever be free.
"Our forefathers gave their lives for us and look at what we have
given them in return. Excuses! We have more excuses than a school's
attendance office for not uniting.
"We continue to rob and steal from one another and kill each
other! We want benefits on plantations called Corporate America, instead
of rebuilding Black Wall Street! We are not building each other up, but
destroying one another like crabs in a barrel," Malcolm continued to
speak into his megaphone in front of the crowd of three hundred students
chanting:
"The power is in the people."
"Police are shooting us down like dogs in the streets with no
accountability. This has been going on for decades. Justice? There's no
justice for the Black man! Police murders caught on tape, red-handed, but
it doesn't matter. We don't matter until we matter to each other!"

The shootings of Trayvon Martin, Tamir Rice, Mike Brown, and
the latest death of Sandra Bland and Korryn Gaines sparked a late-night
rally of police awareness and policing Black communities.
Malcolm was in his last year at Harvard University. He was
known as a militant and was very outspoken about the injustices of Black
people. He was nicknamed "X" for Malcolm X, but Malcolm was his
own man. He didn't adhere to anyone, nor belong to any religious group.
He didn't believe in religion and felt that it was a weapon used against
the Black community to remain slaves. He was a free thinker, a
researcher, and a great orator.

"Mommy, when are we leaving? I'm cold," Tyler said.

"Michelle, do you want me to take him home so you can stay?"

"No, I can take him. You stay. I know this rally is very important to you."

"Are you sure?"

"Of course. Girl, I got this."

"Let's go, little fellow," Michelle said as she grabbed Tyler's hand and walked toward the car to get him out of the cold weather.

It had been over four years since the dreadful March night when Tianna was rushed to Massachusetts General Hospital in critical condition. The attack by her ex-boyfriend Mark White nearly cost her life. She lost so much blood that she had to have a transfusion. She was on bed rest for a month before she began her physical therapy. She had a five-inch scar at the crown of her head that required seventy-five stitches. Thankfully, the scar couldn't be seen because of her thick and coily natural hair. Her rehabilitation from her injuries forced her to take medical leave from school in the spring and fall semesters.

As far as Mark White, he was currently serving five years in prison for aggravated assault. His sentence was a slap on the wrist, and he should've been serving life for what he did to Tianna. She was unable to make the court appearance to testify against him because of her severe injuries.

Mark's parents who were well-known lawyers and highly regarded in the community, boded well for his sentencing. The attack made the national news and caused an uproar about the injustices and violence against Black women. Many felt that Mark's family had paid the judge off for his light sentencing.

Physically, Tianna had made a miraculous recovery, but she struggled mentally. She had nightmares, panic attacks, and often woke up with night sweats. She had been seeing a therapist to help repair her mental state, but it would never again be what it was before the attack.

Dr. Isaac Washington met with Tianna once a week. She had gotten better, but the idea of Mark's early release for good behavior held her hostage. She feared him and his family and knew that she hadn't seen the last of him. He'd sent her many letters from prison throughout the years. Some of the letters she opened, but many of them she burned. Tianna wanted no part of Mark. What he'd done to her was unforgettable and would remain unforgiven. Each time she combed her hair or looked at the scars left on her body, she sighed.

She lost her job at Mark's parents' law firm, which wasn't a surprise. They took their son's side in the incident despite the vicious attack against her. Mark and his family had ruined her character and would do everything in their power to make sure that she didn't receive another internship or employment at any law firms in Massachusetts. So far, they had been successful. They didn't want to face the fact that their son was a violent abuser and monster. His twin sister Markette claimed that if Tianna hadn't cheated on Mark with her high school boyfriend, Jackson Norwood, then none of this would have happened.
It was a case of the perpetrators blaming the victim for his actions.

Tianna's mother Bernadette wanted to bring Tianna home after the attack, but she wanted to stay to finish school. She was carrying a secret from within, and if she had gone back home, the secret would've been revealed. She isolated herself from her family, and her best friend, Tasha Norwood. Tasha often called Tianna to check on her, but Tianna would tell her roommates Michelle and Malcolm to say that she wasn't there or she was busy. After months of giving Tasha the cold shoulder, her phone calls became less frequent to non-existent. This was the way Tianna wanted it.
She wanted no contact with her friends and family in Texas, and that included her fiancé, Jackson.

Tianna hadn't spoken to or seen Jackson since the night of the violent attack when he drove off in his car after finding out that Mark was of a different race. No one had ever seen Mark and they assumed that he was Black. Tianna has never shown any interest in dating outside her race, and to see Mark in the flesh was too much for Jackson to bear. He had never called Tianna, even when Tasha told him about the attack. He wanted to call her, but his anger and hurt kept him away. He thought about killing Mark, but Tasha and his father Adonis talked him off the ledge and told him to let justice take its course. Jackson's emotions were all over the place. He loved Tianna, but he had too much pride to take her back. Their engagement and plans to marry after Tianna finished school were no longer an option or even an afterthought. It was technically over, even though his silence said it wasn't *officially* over.

Jackson didn't make it to the NBA. Instead, he'd finished pharmacy school and was currently working as a pharmacist. He was in the process of opening his own independently owned pharmacy for underprivileged Black people who couldn't afford the expensive prescriptions drugs without insurance.

Jamal heard about the attack on Tianna and took leave from school to be with her. She welcomed only him by her side, but as soon as she was released from the hospital, she sent him on his way so that he could prepare to enter the NBA draft.

Jamal was drafted #1 overall to the San Antonio Spurs. He sent Tianna ten thousand dollars a month to pay for her living expenses. Her scholarship paid for her schooling. Jamal bought her a red BMW and had taken care of her since the incident. He traveled to see Tianna whenever he was in town or during the off-season. He was the only one who knew about her secret other than her mother and grandmother. He promised Tianna that he wouldn't say a word and that *they* would get through it together. Jamal loved Tianna no matter the circumstance and would do anything for her.

There was a knock on the front door and Michelle got off the sofa to answer it. She opened the door.

"Hey, sexy," Michelle said as she moved out of the pathway to let him inside the 3500-square-foot home.

"Daddy, Daddy!" Tyler shouted excitedly as Jamal walked inside the house.

Jamal grabbed Tyler, picked him up in the air, and turned him around like a basketball spinning on his finger.

Tyler yelled, "More, more, Daddy!"

Jamal continued to spin Tyler around and playfully tickled and roughed him up.

"What you been up to, son?"

"Nothing Daddy. I saw you on TV last night."

"Oh, yeah?"

"Yeah, I saw you make the ball into the basket a lot of times. So many times that I lost count."

"Hey, I thought you were keeping track of Daddy's points?"

"I was, but I can only count to forty. Mommy is teaching me to count higher but I get mixed up."

Tianna came into the living room where Jamal was playing with Tyler and gave him a grandiose hug and smile.

She told Jamal how he was ballin' against the Knicks. And that she couldn't wait to see him play tomorrow night against the Celtics.

Tianna, Tyler, Michelle, and X had front row seats to the game. Courtesy of Jamal's privileges in the NBA.

"Where's X?" Jamal asked.

"You know Malcolm X is hardly ever home. He's out fighting for our rights, daily," Michelle said.

"Is he going to make it to the game tomorrow night?"

"Yeah, he will be there cheering for the Celtics."

"I can't wait because I'm going to drop fiddy on his boys!" Jamal bragged as he demonstrated his jump shot.

Michelle and Tianna laughed and shook their heads. They knew how passionate X was about his Boston Celtics. He had been a fan since their last championship against the Lakers. He was too young to remember the Larry Bird era.

"Tianna, you want to catch a movie tonight or go out to the carnival? We can take Tyler with us."

"You don't want to rest and get a massage?" Tianna asked.

"Yeah, you don't want to ice up, son?" Michelle teased Jamal as she patted him on his backside.

"ICE UP, SON," was a reference that NFL player Steve Smith used against another player.

Michelle had been very flirty with Jamal ever since she was introduced to him four years ago. Tianna has never said anything because she and Jamal were just friends, but lately her behavior had gotten on Tianna's last nerve. Tianna was a little jealous. Jamal was single, so technically he was a good-looking bachelor and available. Even though he was single, he saw himself dedicated and devoted to Tianna. He was waiting for her to graduate. She wanted an Ivy League education. And he planned to take her away from Massachusetts as soon as she finished school.

"I want to go to the carnival and ride the merry-go-round," Tyler begged.

"I want to go so Jamal can win me one of those gigantic teddy bears that I can cuddle and sleep with. I'll name him Jamal Jr." Michelle teased.

Jamal often ignored Michelle. He had never cared for bold and aggressive women. It was a turn-off. He hadn't changed much at all since high school. He continued to stay humble despite his good looks and fame. He was down-to-earth Jamal like he always had been, and that's what Tianna loved about him. He didn't let the money or fame change him.

When he signed his contract with the Spurs, he bought his mom a new home and car. He purchased himself a Ford 250 truck and that was it. He lived with his mother when he was in San Antonio, Texas. He hadn't bought a home yet. He was waiting until he was married.

He signed a twenty-million-dollar shoe contract with Nike when he entered the National Basketball Association. He invested his money in CDs, stocks, and bonds. Jamal was smart and frugal with his money, and you would never hear about him filing for bankruptcy after his basketball career ended.

Tianna gave Michelle a look that meant "cool it," Jamal wanted to take *her* to the carnival. Michelle caught her drift and excused herself to the kitchen to fix a grilled cheese sandwich. She asked if anyone wanted one and Tyler was the only one to answer yes. But Tianna said that he couldn't have one because it made him too constipated. He was lactose intolerant.

Jamal and Tyler went into the playroom where Jamal had decor with an indoor basketball court and posters of him with the Spurs organization. He began teaching Tyler how to properly grasp the basketball and how to dribble it. He picked Tyler up so that he could dunk it into his three-foot basketball goal.

All that could be heard from the playroom was laughter and Tyler's soft voice saying, "Daddy, this, and Daddy that."

"You know you need to go ahead and marry that man before he gets away. I don't know what you are waiting for," Michelle said as she walked out of the kitchen with her grilled cheese sandwich and into the living room to sit next to Tianna on the sofa.

"I have school and it's complicated. You wouldn't understand."

"Oh, I fully understand. I understand that if you don't hurry up and marry him that he will find someone else and you are going to regret it. You know how he feels about you."

"I know. I love him, too. It's just that…"

"Let me guess, Jackson?! Girl, you need to get over Jackson Norwood. He ain't thinking about you. You see he hasn't called or tried to contact you since the attack. It's time to move on."

"Yeah, I guess so. You are right. And that's why I love you. You always talk sense into my warped emotions." Tianna pondered the situation further as Michelle hugged her to let her know that she always had her best interest at heart and wanted the best for her.

Even though Tianna knew that she needed to move on from Jackson because it's been over four years since their love affair, she couldn't. She refused to.

Chapter Two

It was a beautiful night in downtown Boston. The lights from the carnival rides looked like Disney World. Tianna, Tyler, and Jamal arrived just before six p.m. Tyler was so excited that he kept running around the Ferris wheel, while Jamal and Tianna were trying to keep ahold of him. He didn't want either of them holding his hand.

"Let go my hand, Daddy. I'm a big boy."

"Oh, yeah?"

"Yes, watch me, Daddy."

Tyler pulled his hand away from Jamal and took off running again.

He disappeared around the corner of the Ferris Wheel but didn't come back out. Tianna turned around and didn't see him. She called his name, but no answer.

Jamal began to call his name too, but no answer.

Tianna panicked and told Jamal to go one way to look and she would go the other way.

They each began looking for Tyler to no avail.

Tianna met up with Jamal with tears and panic across her face.

"I knew I shouldn't have let go of his hand. Please, God, help me find him."

Tianna told Jamal that she was going to contact security. Jamal said that he would continue to look for him and for her to calm down. He would find him.

When Tianna walked up to a security guard standing at the front entrance of the carnival, a familiar voice said, "There's my mommy!"

When Tianna turned toward Tyler's voice, she saw a face that she hadn't seen in over four years. The person held Tyler's hand.

"Tianna?"

"How do you know my mommy?" Tyler asked.

Tianna looked into her eyes. She wanted to take Tyler's hand and run, but she couldn't. She didn't know what to do. The best she could muster was, "Ummmm, thank you."

"Thank you? Girl, quit acting like you don't know me," Tasha said. "Is this your son?" Tasha was still holding Tyler's hand.

"Yes, he's my son."

"Why didn't you tell me you had a son? I mean, who's the father?"

"There's my Daddy!" Tyler said when he saw Jamal.

Tasha turned to see who Tyler was referring to and she looked as though she saw a ghost as she mouthed in slow motion, "Jamal?"

Tianna and Jamal looked at each other and then back at Tasha. They weren't prepared to answer any questions about their son nor had they expected to see Tasha in Boston after all these years.

Tianna wondered what Tasha was doing there, but didn't ask. She couldn't because she had been dissing Tasha soon after the attack. She didn't have the rights to ask her questions since they were no longer close.

After using the gentlemen's room, Darren came from around the corner to meet Tasha. He saw Tianna and Jamal.

"Heyyyyy, what up T and Jamal? What y'all doing here? And who's this little guy?"

"I'm Tyler!"

"Hi, Tyler. It's nice to meet you. I'm Darren and this is my wife, Tasha." Darren said as he shook Tyler's hand.

"Wife?" Tianna mumbled under her breath.

"Hey man, congratulations!" Jamal said. "Why wasn't I invited to the wedding?"

"I tried to contact you, but you changed your number and it was during the playoffs last season. I knew you were trying to get that championship ring."

Darren took Jamal to the side away from Tianna and Tasha and told him that he heard about the attack and asked if Tianna was good. Jamal assured him that she was fine and that he has been by her side since the incident.

Darren had so many questions to ask but decided not to. He was sure Tasha could answer them all soon.

He and Jamal exchanged phone numbers by Jamal calling Darren's phone. Jamal invited him and Tasha to the game the next night if they were still in town.

Darren said that they would be though they were leaving soon. He and Tasha had come to finish a business contract he had with a software company they were trying to buy.

They talked about basketball and caught up on their lives. They made plans to visit each other and keep in touch.

Tianna and Tasha talked and made plans for them all to go to dinner later. They had a lot of catching up to do and a lot of questions that needed to be answered about Tyler.

Chapter Three

Darren and Tasha arrived at the restaurant earlier than Jamal and Tianna. They sat at the table in the back corner of Poetic's restaurant and talked about why Tianna didn't tell her about her and Jamal's relationship, and especially about their son, Tyler. She expressed to Darren how much Tianna had changed, that the Tianna she grew up with wouldn't have a child without being married. Tasha had seen Bernadette a few days before they flew to Boston and asked her about Tianna. Her mother never mentioned that she had a child.

Darren had the same thoughts. He had known Jamal for a long time. He was a man with strong family morals and Darren couldn't understand why they weren't married. Jamal was a professional basketball player and certainly could afford it. Something wasn't right.

When Tasha found Tyler wandering around the carnival all by himself, she wondered what kind of mother would leave a small child without any supervision. When Tyler said that Tianna was his mother, she seemed distanced as if she wanted to run and hide.

Tasha thought about how Tianna had kept her relationship with her brother, Jackson a secret. If she hadn't seen them kissing with her own two eyes, she would never have known about them. Tianna not answering her phone or returning her calls shortly after the attack was unusual as well. She hadn't spoken with or seen her in over four years. Tasha was putting everything together like a private investigator. Tianna didn't want to see her because she was hiding something, and that something was Tyler. *But why would she hide Tyler from her?* Tasha pondered.

Tianna and Jamal entered the restaurant and saw Darren and Tasha waiting for them. Darren saw them come in and signaled. They met at the table where Jamal took Tianna's coat and set it next to his jacket on an extra chair.

"Where's Tyler?" Tasha asked.

"He was getting cranky and tired so we left him with my roommate, Michelle. She'll give him a bath and put him to bed."

"So, how old is he? And how come you never told us about him?" Tasha got straight to the point. She wasn't beating around the bush. She wanted answers and she wanted to know *now*.

"Babe, let's just order our food first and then we all can talk," Darren whispered to Tasha.

Tasha hissed. She did what her husband asked, but she wasn't going to leave the restaurant without any answers.

Darren continued to lighten the mood by talking about everything other than Tyler. He talked mostly about Jamal and the Spurs. Tasha sat there eyeing Tianna's every move. Tianna was fidgeting like she was on trial for murder. Obviously she wasn't, but she had some explaining to do and she knew that Tasha wasn't going to go away quietly.

"So, how long have you and Jamal been together?"

Tianna grabbed Jamal's hand and they looked into each other's eyes and answered in unison.

"Four years," Tianna said.

"Five years," Jamal said with uncertainty.

They weren't prepared to answer questions about their non-relationship. They were not together. In fact, they remained friends without benefits.

"Which one is it, four or five years?" Tasha asked as though she was irritated and knew they both were lying.

"We've been friends for so long, we lost track, but Jamal is right. It's been five years."

"Five years and a baby and y'all ain't married?" Tasha asked as though she didn't believe a word they said.

"Yeah, man, y'all got a son and we are baffled that you two love birds haven't tied the knot."

When Tianna was about to respond, she heard Tasha's phone ring. Tasha looked down and saw her brother calling. She answered on the second ring.

"Hey, what's up, Jackson?"

Hearing Jackson's name and knowing he was on the phone made Tianna's heart palpitate. She wanted so badly to grab Tasha's phone to see how he was doing and to tell him how much she still loved him. She thought back on their time spent together and how much she missed him.

"Yeah, guess who I'm having dinner with?" Tasha spoke into the phone.

Tianna began to sweat. She was so nervous that she had to excuse herself and go to the ladies' room. Jamal stood up to pull her chair out. When she got there, she began to throw up. She went into the bathroom stall and let it rip. She threw up her dinner. She got down on both knees to hover over the toilet seat and began to cry.
She cried for about five minutes. She opened the bathroom stall and saw Tasha standing outside it with her hands on her hips.

"What's going on with you, Tianna? Why have you been avoiding me for over four years? I finally see you, and you and Jamal have a four-year-old son!"

"Tasha, please don't start with all the questions. I haven't been avoiding you. It's just that the attack has taken its toll on me."

Tianna washed her hands and face, she pulled out her travel size toothbrush, toothpaste, and mouthwash to brush her teeth while Tasha stood there wondering who the woman was standing next to her.

Tianna looked into the mirror and applied her compact powder and lip-gloss.

Tasha didn't know whether to be more sympathetic and believe Tianna because she lied to her before about her relationship with Jackson. She knew for a fact that Tianna and Jackson were together. Her brother confessed and told her everything.

Tasha decided to change the subject for now and she and Tianna talked about Mark and his imprisonment. She made Tasha aware that he was due to be released soon. She told her about the letters she had received from him.
She asked Tianna to move back home with her to get away from Mark and so she could be a part of Tyler's life. How she would love to be his Godmother.

Tasha told her about seeing her mother and asked if Bernadette knew about Tyler. Tianna told her that she did know about him.

She asked Tianna Tyler's age again and she said that's he was four years old. She asked his birthdate and she told her September fifteenth.

She told Tianna that Jackson asked about her when she talked to him on the phone. Tianna could hardly think knowing this. She wanted to confess her love for Jackson, but she resisted. It wasn't the time or place.

Tianna and Tasha walked back to the restaurant table, and Jamal and Darren were laughing and reminiscing about high school. They hardly noticed the ladies' return, they were having so much fun. They both stood up to pull out their chairs to be seated.

"Is everything okay?" Jamal asked Tianna.

She kissed Jamal gently on the lips to assure him that everything was fine.

It was getting late and Jamal had to return to the team's hotel room before curfew.

He told Darren and Tasha that tickets would be at the box office if they decided to go to the game.

Tasha and Tianna made plans to get together before they left town. Tianna promised to have Tasha for lunch at her home before her return to Texas.

Chapter Four

Primetime game night on TNT network, the San Antonio Spurs vs. the Boston Celtics.

Ernie Johnson, Kenny Smith, Shaquille O'Neil, and Charles Barkley talk about the dynasty of the Spurs. Charles Barkley had to give his opinion about the women in San Antonio and how overweight they are. Every time the Spurs were on national TV he made reference to the River Walk, its dirty water, and the big women.

Barkley had a point, there were a lot of overweight women in San Antonio, but it was no different than any other city. Obesity was widespread. Kenny Smith let him know that he needed to lose weight too, and stop talking about the beautiful women in San Antonio, Texas. He stated how much he loved the city and how hospitable the people were when he visited.

Tianna, Michelle, Malcolm X, and Tyler arrived at TD Garden arena wearing their Spurs paraphernalia. Tianna and Tyler wore #1, Jamal's jersey number. Michelle wore Tim Duncan's jersey. Malcolm wore his Isaiah Thomas jersey. As soon as they sat down, a rude drunk Celtics fan began heckling Tianna and Michelle.

"Boooo. Go back to San Antonio."

"Shut yo drunk ass up!" Michelle said.

"Hey man, chill the hell out! Leave these women alone." X retorted.

Malcolm exchanged seats with Michelle so that he could sit next to the heckler. He was going to protect his Black woman at all cost. He referred to Black women as goddesses.

When X changed seats with Michelle, the drunk heckler didn't say another word.

Jamal ran onto the basketball court to warm-up along with the rest of his team. As soon as Tyler saw Jamal, he yelled,

"There goes my Daddy!" He began calling for Jamal.

Jamal heard Tyler calling him and ran over to their seats to give Tyler some dap and speak to Tianna, Michelle, and X.

"Yo, X, I'm glad you could make it. Watch me drop fiddy on yo boys!"

"We betting a thousand or what?"

"Make it two-thousand!"

"Thanks for the courtside seats, Jamal!"

Jamal winked and said he would see them after the game.

"Bye Daddy! Good luck!" Tyler wished.

When Jamal turned around he saw Darren and Tasha looking for their seats. He whistled to Darren to get his attention. They saw Jamal and he pointed to their row. Tianna waved to them. They found their seats right next to Tianna and Tyler.

"Hi, Mrs. Tasha and Mr. Darren!" Tyler greeted them both.

"Hello Tyler, you are so sweet and well mannered," Tasha said as she sat right next to Tyler while taking off her jacket and hanging it on the back of her seat.

"Mommy, can I have some cotton candy?"

"You need to eat something first before you get any sweets. Do you want a hot dog or hamburger?"

"Hot dog!"

"Let's go get you a hot dog. I will be right back," Tianna told Michelle and Tasha.

"Tianna, let me take him to get a hot dog." Tasha reiterated.

"Tasha, are you sure? I want to keep ahold of him. You remember what happened at the carnival last night. I turned my back for a second and he was gone."

"Girl, I know, and I assure you, I will hold on to him tight."

Tianna reluctantly let Tyler go with Tasha. They were back within twenty minutes. Tyler sat eating his hot dog and finished with his cotton candy.

Tasha kept looking at Tyler the entire night instead of watching the game. Tianna noticed how she kept watching Tyler as well.

"My daddy has forty-eight points. That's almost fifty. Right, mommy?"

"Yes, that's right," Tasha said.

"Uncle, X, you're going to owe my daddy two thousand dollars."

"Boy, you are too smart for your britches. Your daddy still needs two points and it's only two minutes remaining in the game."

The Spurs were down by one point with eighteen seconds remaining in the game.

Jamal dribbled the ball down the court with five seconds left.

"Shoot it, Daddy! Shoot it!" Tyler yelled.

Jamal imagined hearing his son telling him to shoot and he did what Tyler told him. He was at the three-point line when he let it fly. The ball hit the rim and the buzzer sounded as it dropped into the basket. Tyler, Tianna, Tasha, Darren, Michelle, and even X jumped to their feet to cheer. They began giving each other high fives and shouting Jamal's name.

"Daddy, you did it!" Tyler began to count on his fingers. "Forty-eight, forty-nine, ummmm, forty-eight, forty-nine... Fifty! Fifty-one!"

Michelle looked at X and said, "well, there goes your rent money and car payment. You should never bet against Jamal."

Tianna assured X that Jamal would probably waive the bet, so he shouldn't worry about it. X thought to himself, *a bet is a bet, and he's a man, and a man always pays.* Even if Jamal waived the bet, X would still insist on paying.

Jamal looked into the stands, winked, and raised his fist to his son.

They cheered and so did the crowd.

The heckler that booed Tianna and Michelle threw his can of beer at one of the Spurs players but missed. The security guard at the door saw the heckler and came over to escort him out in handcuffs. He began cursing and shouting all kinds of racial slurs at the security guard. A police officer was called in on the scene after the man became more and more aggressive.

"Mommy, what's wrong with that man? Is he mad because the Celtics lost?" Tyler asked.

"Yes, and he had too much to drink," Tianna answered.

"That fool needs to go to jail!" Michelle said.

Tianna wished that neither Michelle nor Malcolm would say anything, especially with her son with them. She held onto his hand tight and continued walking through the crowd as fast as she could to get away from the heckler.

"Tianna, slow down!" Tasha called, but she continued walking because she didn't hear her.

Tasha grabbed Tianna's arm and spun her around. For some reason, Tianna thought it was the heckler so she began yelling, "Let go of me!"

"It's me—Tasha!"

Tianna clenched her chest and told Tasha not to scare her like that. Tasha apologized and explained that she only wanted to confirm their lunch date for tomorrow. She didn't mean to startle her. Tianna set a time to meet at her home and they embraced each other to say good night.

Tasha kissed Tyler and said her farewells to Michelle and X, and she and Darren left to acquire their rental car.

"Are you okay? You look like you saw a ghost," Michelle said.

"Yes, I'm fine. I just need to get out of here."

The truth was, Tianna wasn't fine. During the time the heckler was escorted out of the arena, she thought she saw a gentleman that looked just like Mark. She knew he was due to be released soon, but she didn't know his release date. The state is supposed to give victims a fourteen-day notice when offenders are released but Tianna didn't get a notice.

"I'll get the car, you and Michelle can wait here," X said. X pulled up to the curb of TD arena in his Ford Explorer to escort Tianna, Tyler, and Michelle home safely.

Chapter Five

*M*ark, *please don't hurt us. I'm sorry. I wanted to tell you, but I didn't know how. Please don't hurt Tyler. He's all I've got. Please. If there's any reconciliation between you and me, we can get counseling to help us pull through it. Please take the knife away from his throat. Please!*

Mark, Noooooooo! Tianna begged.

"Mommy, Mommy! Are you okay?" Tyler said as he entered Tianna's bedroom to see his mother's hair all disheveled and her nightgown drenched. Her face dripped with sweat and eyes poured with tears like a water faucet. Her chest heaved like she was on a treadmill running twenty miles per hour. She brushed her hair out of her face with her hand, but it fell back into place like it was marching in line for a drill sergeant. She grabbed the bottle of Fuji water that sat next to her bed for her anxiety medications. She opened the bottle of Xanax, popped the water top, and took a pill. She drank uncontrollably like she hadn't tasted water in years.

Tyler stood there in his Spiderman pajamas wiping his sleepy eyes waiting for his mother to answer him. She finally did.

"I'm okay, baby. Let's get you back to bed."

"Mommy, can I sleep with you?"

Tianna didn't want Tyler sleeping with her because she wanted to make sure that he didn't see her in her most vulnerable stages of the nightmares. She had gone from having only one nightmare a month to having them almost nightly. She felt Mark's presence everywhere she went. She was at the study hall and she thought she heard his voice. It was a classmate. She walked to the bookstore and saw a guy wearing a leather jacket like the one Mark wore on their first date. The physical and mental scars drained the life out of her soul.

She talked with her therapist, but he just increased her anxiety medications and set their meetings to twice a week. She'd regressed from where she was a few months ago.

Her nightmares were the reason Jamal slept in the guestroom when he visited. She was too embarrassed to reveal her panics attacks to him. No one knew how much she suffered in silence.
She hid it well. When anyone asked how she was doing, her answer was always, "I'm doing great!"

Tianna reluctantly let Tyler sleep with her that night. She stayed awake reading the autobiography, *The Ghetto Blues* written by a local author from her hometown, San Antonio, Texas. *The Ghetto Blues* was a captivating story of a young woman that experienced many obstacles in her life but never gave up the fight to escape the mental abuse of her environment. Tianna looked at her life and could relate to the book. She waited until her son was breathing deeply and then she turned off the lamp and fell asleep too.
They awoke the next morning to Jamal's voice.
"Daddy, is that you?"
"Yes, son. I've come to take you with me before I leave town. I have some of your things packed already. I want you to get dressed so that we can let your mom sleep in."
"Jamal, I'm awake. You don't have to take him if you don't want to. You need to get some rest yourself before heading to Denver."

The Spurs had a four-day stretch before they were back on the road to play the Nuggets. Coach Pop gave them a day off from practice and Jamal wanted to spend time with Tyler and Tianna, but he overheard her having nightmares while sleeping in the guestroom. He wanted to come into her bedroom to comfort her, but he didn't want her to know that he knew about the nightmares. He waited for her to reveal it to him. He thought about killing Mark, too for what he did to her. He said Mark was lucky that the justice system was protecting him. Because Mark's mother would need a new black dress for his burial.
Jamal wasn't a hostile man, but he would do anything to protect his family. He considered Tianna his family and of course his son, Tyler, too.
"Can Mommy come with us?"
"No, Mommy is going to wait for Tasha and we are going for lunch. I will be fine," Tianna said.
"Are you sure?"

"Yes, I'm sure." She kissed Tyler softly on his cheek.

"Now, go with Daddy so he can help you brush your teeth."

"Mrs. Tasha already brushed my teeth last night at the game. Why do I have to brush them again?"

Tianna and Jamal said simultaneously, "What?"

They asked Tyler to repeat himself and to get the details of Tasha brushing his teeth and most importantly, why was she brushing his teeth? What Tyler told them didn't make any sense. Tianna decided that she would ask her about what Tyler said as soon as she met her for lunch.

Tianna's doorbell rang and she looked through the peephole to see Tasha standing on the other side. She was looking cute with her pink Gucci sweat suit and glasses. She wore pink sneakers with white and pink shoelaces.

Tianna opened the door and let her inside. Tasha stepped in and asked what was that smell. Tianna explained that it was Michelle burning incense.

"Where's Tyler?" Tasha asked.

"He's with Jamal. They are spending time together before he leaves for Denver. Speaking of Tyler. He told me that you brushed his teeth when we were at the game last night. Is there a reason why you did that?"

Tasha was caught off guard and didn't know how to answer. So, she said that he was eating cotton candy and with all that sugar, she didn't want it to damage his enamel.

Tianna didn't buy that response since Tyler hadn't eaten cotton candy. She just said "Ooh" for the sake of argument. What Tasha did was put Tianna's senses on high alert to see what she was up to.

"You ready to go?"

"Yes, let me get my keys," Tianna said as she grabbed them and told Michelle that she was leaving.

Tianna's Candy Apple BMW sat in the driveway shining. Tasha admired the convertible and asked when she purchased it. Tianna explained how Jamal bought it for her soon after he signed his contract with Nike. Tasha asked why she and Jamal weren't married but Tianna made the excuse that it was because of school.

Tasha asked if her mom and grandmother knew about Tyler. She was asking this for the second time. Tianna told her again that they did, and she and Tyler were planning a trip to Texas. Tasha made plans with her and Tyler when she came to Texas. She looked forward to getting Tianna back into her life like when they were younger; she missed her so much.

Tasha caught Tianna up with what had been going on in her life. She confessed to her how she and Darren wanted to start a family sooner rather than later. They made small talk during and after lunch.

The one person that Tianna didn't want to talk about was Jackson or maybe she did? She was happy that Tasha hadn't mentioned him the entire time. Every time Tasha's phone rang, she prayed that it wasn't him. Tasha mentioned her mother, Sharon, and father, Adonis but not her brother.

Tianna wanted to ask about Jackson, but she refrained. She wanted to know why he hadn't called to check on her in years. She wondered if Tasha told him about Tyler. She hoped not, but she knew her friend and would place money on a bet that Jackson knew about Tyler.

She wanted to tell Jackson about him, but she felt abandoned as if he'd left her for dead. If it wasn't for Tasha, she would have died. Jackson wasn't responsible for what Mark did but they were engaged at the time of the incident. He left and never looked back. She still kept the ring he gave her in a special place in her heart and in her room. It was in a small locked safe box with a picture of her and Jackson and the necklace he gave her for Christmas. She didn't know how long it would be before her heart let him go. Her mind wanted to, but her heart was stubborn as a mule.

"So, has my brother tried to contact you?" Tasha asked. Tianna was stunned that Tasha would bring up Jackson the moment her mind was on him. It was like she read her thoughts.

"No, why would he?" Tianna responded. She tried to play the acting role to perfection, but she failed miserably.

"Tianna, I know that you and Jackson had something going on. Let's get it out in the open. We are not teenagers anymore. I know that you love him, and he loves you."

Tianna didn't know how to respond. She wanted to come clean with all the secrets. She let a teardrop roll down her cheek because thinking about him made her cry. She couldn't hold it inside any longer.

"I'm going to tell Jackson about you and Jamal, *and* Tyler," Tasha said.

Tianna took a gulp of her saliva. "Why would you do such a thing? Tasha, I wish you would not step over the boundaries of our friendship and let me handle things my way."

"I've tried letting you handle things your way. If I hadn't seen you at the carnival I still wouldn't know about Tyler. He's *four* years old," Tasha retorted.

"You're right, but things are so complicated. I have a lot of things going on in my life right now. I just need to finish school and things will settle down and become as normal as possible."

Tasha didn't say much afterward and let Tianna know of her plans to leave town that night. She and Darren were flying back home. She assured Tianna that she was there for her no matter what. If she needed anything, she wanted her to call and not hesitate. She loved and missed her and wanted her back in her life. Especially since Tyler was a part of her life now.

They drove back to Tianna's home and said their goodbyes. Tianna watched Tasha drive away.

She walked inside her home and felt an emptiness. She already missed her best friend.

Chapter Six

Tasha walked inside the DNA reference laboratory in San
Antonio and handed the lab assistant a plastic bag with a toothbrush
inside. She then provided a swab of her own DNA. She was advised that
the results would be back within three days.

She then drove into town to visit her brother at work. She walked
inside the pharmacy and watched her brother refill prescriptions and
counsel patients picking up their medicine. When he was done with the
clients, she stood at the counter. Jackson saw her and smiled.

"Hey, you, what you doing here?"

"Nothing, I can't come by and see how my big brother is doing?"

"Tasha, I know you. So just spill it."

"Welllll, if *you* insist. I just came back from Boston and I saw
Tianna and she's had a major life change."

Jackson's smile vanished instantly, as if he had just been struck
by lightning. He looked away and then said, "How is she?"

"She's doing good. She and her son, Tyler."

"Son? Tasha what are you talking about."

"Yeah, she has a four-year-old son by Jamal."

Jackson's heart dropped hearing son, Tianna, and Jamal in the
same sentence. He stared into space until a pharmacy technician,
Roxanne, called for him to counsel a client about her prescription.

Jackson told her that he will be right there. He bid his sister
farewell and told her that they would finish their conversation later.
She reached to give her brother a kiss on the cheek and told him that she
would see him in three days.

"Hey babe, are you okay? Who was that girl?" Roxanne asked.

"That was my sister, Tasha."

"What did she say? It looks like you just saw a ghost."

"Nothing. Are we still getting together tonight?" he asked.

"Of course, and I can hardly wait," she said as she kissed Jackson
and gave him a pat on his backside.

Jackson and Roxanne had been seeing each other for about two
months. He hadn't introduced her to the family yet because he didn't

know how serious their relationship was. The next woman he would bring home to meet his family would be the woman he intended to marry. He didn't know if Roxanne was marriage material. She probably was, but he still loved Tianna. The hurt and pain of her being with Mark kept him away.

He thought about her the entire day, and the fact that she had a son with *Jamal*.

Later that night, Roxanne showed up at Jackson's home.

"Babe, what's wrong? You haven't been your jovial self since the visit from your sister. When will I meet your family anyway?"

"We've only been together for two months. I told you the next woman I bring home to meet my family will be my wife."

"Oh, so what are we doing then?"

"What you mean? We're screwing right now, so let's not ruin the mood," Jackson said as he turned Roxanne over to kiss her shoulder, neck, and back.

He needed a release after what he'd heard about Tianna. He tried to get his mind off her, but he couldn't. When Roxanne visited, he welcomed her inside and made her feel as comfortable as could be, but she felt the distance. His body was there with her but his mind was somewhere else. And she was right, his mind was in Boston, Massachusetts.

Tasha returned to the DNA reference laboratory after receiving a phone call that the results of the testing were in. She hurried to get the results, driving through traffic like a madwoman to get to the laboratory before the close of the business day. She opened the sealed envelope and read the number of centimorgans that Tyler and her DNA contained. The results read that they shared 1,688 centimorgans across 77 segments.

Tasha called Darren on the phone immediately and told him that she would be home a little late that night. She was going to visit her brother. She told him not to wait up for her and hung up the phone even before he had a chance to ask why. She was on a mission.

Chapter Seven

The airplane arrived at Logan's International airport at approximately six thirty p.m.

Jackson made plans to have a rental car waiting for him. He retrieved the rental and placed his luggage inside the trunk.

He stopped at a local restaurant to get a bite to eat since he hadn't eaten all day and his appetite had wavered since hearing the news about Tianna and Jamal having a son together.

Once he was done eating, he hopped in the car and played some old school jazz. He told Siri the address and he was on his way.

Michelle and X were watching the movie, *Malcolm X* directed by Spike Lee when the doorbell rang. Michelle huffed and didn't want to answer it because she didn't want to miss any parts of the movie, although she and X had watched the movie together more than five times.

X told her that he got it. She asked if he wanted to pause the movie, but he said to let it play.

X opened the door without looking through the peephole.

"Yeah, can I help you?"

"Yeah, I'm looking for Tianna," he said, standing there dressed in all black looking like a Black Panther ready to strike.

"She's not here right now."

"Do you know when she'll be back?"

"Man, I don't give out that type of information. Who are you anyway?"

"That's none of your concern. I'll be back in an hour."

X turned and closed the door and mutters, "suit yourself," when Tianna's red BMW pulled into the driveway. She noticed an unfamiliar car and thought it was one of X's friends from school over to study. She parked right next to the car. She opened the back door to get Tyler from his booster seat. He'd fallen asleep on the way home from daycare.

She closed the car door and found him standing within inches of her and Tyler. She jumped when she saw his face. She hadn't seen him in over four years!

"Oh my God! What are you doing here?" she asked, trying not to wake Tyler.

"I've come to see you and to ask you something. Can we go inside?"

"Sure, let me put him to bed and we can talk."

Jackson followed Tianna into the house. She asked Michelle to take Tyler and put him to bed. When Michelle came down from putting Tyler to bed, that's when Tianna formerly introduced everyone.

She and Jackson went out on the balcony where there was a swing, furniture, and decor that sat beautifully in the covered area on a forty-degree night.

Jackson continued staring at Tianna as she walked in front of him. She asked if he wanted something to eat or drink and he said nothing. He wanted to take all of her in. She had changed so much. She'd cut her dreadlocks and was rocking a huge Afro now. She accented it with sparkling hair jewelry. Her ass was fatter than ever but in a good way. She asked him to have a seat, but he didn't. It was like he was in a trance. He said nothing but was on her like a moth to a flame. She tried to maintain some space but he rejected it and kept entering hers. He stood within inches of her when he asked, "Where is Tyler's father?"

"What do you mean? Tianna asked, fumbling over every syllable in each word.

"*Where is Tyler's father?*" he asked again.

"He's in Denver getting ready to play the Nuggets."

"Nawww, let me ask you again," Jackson said. He kept moving closer and closer to her as he backed her into the rails of the balcony which left her nowhere to run.

He lifted her chin and looked into her eyes as his body pressed against hers.

She moved to the side but he followed every step.

Michelle and X peeped onto the balcony at the site of Jackson standing in front of Tianna. Michelle knew their history and wasn't worried, but X wondered if he should go and break them apart and check on Tianna. Michelle said that Tianna was fine. She *loved* Jackson.

They returned to the sofa to watch their movie after Michelle assured X that Tianna was good.

"Jackson, what are you talking about?"

"You know exactly what I'm talking about," he said as he lifted her chin.

"Is Tyler *my* son?"

"What? No, we haven't been together in years. He is Jamal's son." She tried to reason with him and get out of his personal space.

"Oh, is that right? Then why does this tell me that he is?" He asked as he pulled out the DNA reference laboratory results that Tasha gave him.

"What is that?" Tianna asked.

"It's proof that Tyler is *my* son. But I want to hear it from you. Is Tyler my son?"

"Jackson, stop—don't."

"Don't what?"

"Don't complicate things. We have a routine and it will only confuse him."

"Confuse him? That's *my* son. I'm going to get my son!"

Jackson turned away from her and opened the balcony door heading upstairs to wake Tyler.

Tianna grabbed his arm to stop him. She wanted to explain everything to him. Jackson refused at first but reluctantly decided to hear her out.

She told him how he left her for dead and that she didn't know she was pregnant until she was transported to the hospital and regained consciousness. It was a miracle that she hadn't lost him. She said that when he and Tasha visited, she was indeed three months pregnant with his son.

Jackson thought about her gaining a little weight and that he should have known something was off.

He cried in Tianna's arms and apologized profusely for leaving her. He told her about the anger and hurt he felt about seeing Mark and how he wanted to kill him for what he did.

They sat on the balcony and talked for hours. There was laughter, tears, and love shared the entire night. Tianna offered him the guestroom, but he said that he had a hotel. She insisted that he stay. He did, but he wanted to check on his son.

He went inside Tyler's room and sat on his bed and watched him sleep. He stroked his hair and thought about the four years that he'd missed. He missed his first steps, his first words, and his first four birthdays. He made a promise that he wouldn't miss another day.

He kissed Tyler goodnight and he and Tianna closed his door. Tianna led Jackson to the guestroom.

While showing Jackson around her home his cell phone rang and it was Roxanne.

Tianna heard a woman's voice when he answered. His conversation with her was brief, but she heard Roxanne call Jackson babe and say that she loved him. He didn't return the sentiments, but Tianna felt the reason was because she was standing there.

She told Jackson goodnight and as soon as she closed the door, she clenched her stomach and began to cry.

She entered her room, disrobed, and stepped into the shower. She sobbed under the water and afterward in the bed as she cried herself into a deep slumber. She woke up to feel someone getting in her bed and it was Jackson.

She whispered to him, "What are you doing?"

"I couldn't sleep. But don't worry. I won't touch you," he said as he turned on his side and fell asleep. She heard his low snores and thought about the first time they ever made love. It was five years ago on Christmas night when their son was conceived.

Chapter Eight

The Spurs were down by four points with two minutes remaining in the game. They led the Denver Nuggets at half-time by twenty-one points. Jamal Johnson, the leading scorer, had the ball in his hands coming down the court. He passed the ball and it was swung back to him. He tried to avoid a defender, planted his left foot on the floor, and fell to the ground with no contact from another player. He lay on the basketball court holding his left leg.

"Mommy, what's wrong with Daddy?"

Tianna didn't answer. She sat on the couch holding her hand over her mouth fixated on the television and praying for Jamal to get up. He got up, but with assistance as he put his right arm around his teammate and left arm around the trainer. He grimaced in pain. He was taken to the locker room for evaluation.

The sports commentators feared the worst, saying it appeared to be a torn Achilles tendon and he could be done for the season.

Tianna ignored the reports of the sports analysts, praying that it was an ankle sprain and that he would be okay. She wanted to call him but knew that he wouldn't answer since he was probably getting treatment or being evaluated.

Michelle came to put her arm around Tianna to assure her that everything would be okay. Tianna grabbed her son and held him tight because he kept asking and wanting to talk to his daddy.

"I want my daddy!" Tyler continued to cry.

X came to turn off the television so that Tyler couldn't watch or hear the updates on Jamal.

"Tyler, you want to go out for some ice cream?"

"No, I want my daddy. I don't want any ice cream!"

Tyler never turned down lactose free ice cream. When the offer didn't calm him down, Tianna knew it would be a long night.

She took Tyler upstairs and brought her cell phone to see if she could contact Jamal. She dialed his number and it went straight to voicemail. She gave the phone to Tyler so that he could hear Jamal's voicemail and leave him a message.

"Daddy, it's me. Are you okay? I saw you hurt yourself. Please call me back, Daddy. I love you."

As soon as Tyler left his message, he felt better. Tianna was able to give him a bath and put him to sleep. He basically cried himself to sleep. Before he fell asleep and after taking his bath, he called Jamal again but to no avail.

Tianna assured Tyler that his daddy was fine and that she would keep calling. He needed to get some sleep because he had a field trip to the zoo tomorrow at school. She tucked him in, kissed him goodnight, and turned on his night light.

Tianna went downstairs to talk to Michelle and X. She talked about Jamal and Jackson. Jackson was coming by tonight. He was making plans to move to Boston to be closer to his son. He begged Tianna to move back to Texas, but she wanted to finish school. Jackson didn't want to spend another minute out of Tyler's life, so asking him to wait two more years until she graduated was asking too much. He wanted to be a father to his son. Tianna asked that she be allowed to tell Tyler about him on her own time. Jackson didn't want to wait; he wanted his son to know the truth and said he would adapt to the change. Tianna disagreed. They went back and forth on telling Tyler. Jackson reluctantly agreed to give her some time, but he wasn't waiting forever. If she didn't tell him, he would.

He had to tie up some loose ends and made plans to come over later that night to further discuss Tyler, *his* son.

Tianna received a call from Jamal after he'd received the messages from her and Tyler. She was shocked and excited that he called so soon. He filled her in on his prognosis. He would have an MRI in the morning but didn't want them to worry about him. She told him about Tyler and how upset he was. Jamal was saddened that he had already been put to bed. He wanted to talk to his son. He told her that he would call him tomorrow after school.

Tianna hung up the phone and sighed. She was concerned about his injury, but she didn't want to tell him Jackson was in town and wanted a relationship with his son. She didn't like keeping secrets from Jamal, but it was not the right time or place. His injury was more important.

Tianna met Jackson at his hotel room instead of her house. She was uptight about Jamal's injury but wanted to get some fresh air and have a change of scenery. Jackson opened the door in a black t-shirt and black and gray basketball shorts. It looked as though he'd just completed a workout, but his body smelled of Kenneth Cole cologne, so he must have just gotten out of the shower. He wore black socks, but no shoes. The television blasted SportsCenter. There were clips of Jamal's injury plastered all over the sports channels. It was breaking news.

Jackson offered to take Tianna's coat and asked if she had eaten. She didn't have much of an appetite, so she asked for water or lemonade.

"You still love you some lemonade, huh?"

"I can't believe you remembered."

"I remember a lot of things about you."

"Oh really, like what?"

"I noticed the weight you gained; you're wearing it well," he said as he came from behind her to hand her a fresh glass of lemonade. He brushed up against her and the heat from his touch took her back five years. His cologne was intoxicating enough.

"Have a seat. Take your shoes off and make yourself comfortable."

Tianna took a seat on the sofa and made note of how nice the hotel room was.

"So, how long will you be in town?"

"I don't know. I'm trying to do some things so that I can be in my son's life. Where is he, by the way?"

"He's at home sleeping. Michelle and X are with him. He was upset about his father's—I mean *Jamal's* injury, and cried himself to sleep. He is going on a trip to the zoo tomorrow."

Jackson was not particularly concerned about Jamal's injury, but didn't want to see him hurt. He didn't like the fact that Tyler thought Jamal was his father. He didn't want his son calling another man "dad" or "father" when he was the father.

"You mean Jamal? Because I'm his father. And he will know it soon," he said as he grabbed Tianna's foot to take off her shoes.

"What time is he going to the zoo?"

"I think they will arrive at around nine a.m."

"Oh, I got to make a call to my parents to let them know they have a grandson," Jackson said.

"Jackson, do we have to do this right now?"

"Yeah. You had four years to tell me, but you didn't, so yeah, it has to be right now."

He got up to retrieve his phone from the bedroom and came to sit back down on the sofa next to Tianna. He dialed his parents' number and Sharon picked up after the third ring.

"Hey, son, it's good to finally hear from you."

"Hi Mama, is Dad there?"

"Yes, he's right here."

"Can you put me on speaker phone? Tianna and I have something to tell you."

Tianna looked at Jackson and mouthed, "What?" She couldn't believe he was putting her on the spot. He said nothing but continued. His parents were in disbelief because they hadn't heard from Tianna in years and wondered what Jackson was doing with her. They knew about her attack because Adonis had to stop Jackson from wanting to kill Mark.

"Mama, this may come as a shock, but I'm a father!" Jackson said excitedly.

"What? Jackson Jeffrey Norwood, what are you talking about?" his mother asked.

"I'm a father!" he said again as if they didn't hear him the first time. Tianna wanted to disappear. She tried to get up, but Jackson pulled her back and rested his leg on top of hers.

"We heard you, son, but who is the mother and how and when did this happen?" Adonis asked.

"The mother is sitting right here with me, Dad."

Adonis and Sharon said in unison, "Tianna?!"

"Yup, tell them, Tianna," Jackson said as he moved the phone closer to Tianna's mouth to speak.

"Hi, Mrs. and Mr. Norwood. How are you?" Tianna asked nervously.

"We're fine but what's this about you and Jackson having a child together? I mean, we didn't even know you two were together. When did this happen?"

"Well, it's a long story."

She began by telling them about the attack and how she was three months pregnant and how Tyler was a miracle child. She told them everything about him and how smart he was and that she was bringing him down in March during her break. She told them about her and Jackson's secret relationship and the reason it was kept that way because of Tasha's accident. Mrs. Norwood was shocked about everything, but she was excited to see her first grandchild.

Adonis wanted to know one thing and one thing only. "When are Tianna and Jackson getting married?" He taught his son to be a man and to take care of his responsibilities like a man. There was no way that he would have a grandchild but no marriage between his son and Tianna.

"Dad, Tianna and I *are* engaged," he said.

Tianna looked at him and thought to herself: *Is he serious?* This was all new to her. She didn't respond to the engagement comment because "technically" they never broke off the engagement, but since she hadn't heard from Jackson in years, she'd assumed they were no longer together.

"When is the wedding?" Mrs. Norwood asked.

"Soon, Mama, you and Dad will be the first to know. I just wanted to call and let you know that I'm a father and you have a grandson!" he kept saying.

The Norwoods congratulated Tianna and Jackson. They were excited about their grandchild but didn't like the fact that they were not married. They believed in marriage before children. And so did Jackson and Tianna, even though it didn't turn out that way for them. He planned to do right by Tianna and his son.

They bid his parents good night and promised to call them again with Tyler. They wanted to talk to their grandchild. They didn't know how complicated things were with Jamal, Tianna, and Tyler.

As soon as Jackson pushed the end button, Tianna said, "Why on earth would you tell your parents we are engaged?" She walked to the balcony to look out at the city.

"Because we are, and besides *you* know you can't resist me."

"Yes, I can." She swallowed.

"Oh, is that right?" he said as he moved closer to her. She kept backing up, but he kept coming closer.

"Why you moving?"

"Because…"

"Because what?" he said as he licked his lips. She loved and hated when he did that because it drove her crazy like a wild animal locked in a cage. She wanted no part of Jackson Norwood. She tried to reason with herself.

"I'm not playin' with you, Jackson."

"Does it look like I'm playing?" he said as he stepped into her personal space.

She turned to keep from looking at his eyes making love to hers. He walked to get closer to her and wrapped his arms around her waist.

"Jackson, stop."

"Is that a stop meaning *go,* or a stop meaning *caution*?"

"Both…" she mumbled softly.

She couldn't resist him as much as she tried. He tilted her face toward his and her eyes said it all. They said how much she still loved him. He picked her up in his arms and carried her inside, but not only inside, he took her to his bedroom, disrobed her and that's where her "Stop, Jackson" turned into "Don't stop, Jackson."

Chapter Nine

The instructions were given to each of the childcare teachers and chaperones. There were twelve children to each teacher and two chaperones. Ms. Woods, the school's director, asked that Tyler be carefully monitored because of his attention span and his tendency to wander off the minute you turned your head.

Each child wore a name tag along with the name of their school. Tyler wore his father's jersey on top of a long sleeve shirt, a Spurs jacket with black warm-up pants, and his Nike shoes.

His eyes were puffy from crying himself to sleep about Jamal. He didn't want to attend school until after he'd spoken to him. Tianna called Jamal and he let his son know that he was fine and he would be there to see him soon. Tyler was so happy to hear from him. After hearing his voice, he was finally ready to go to school so that he could see the animals at the zoo.

The weather was a breezy sixty-five degrees. It was perfect for a visit to the Franklin Park Zoo.

The children were excited as soon as they arrived. They exited the bus in a single line. Ms. Kathy was responsible for Tyler and eleven other children. She did exactly what Ms. Woods said and kept a close eye on Tyler.

Jackson arrived at Franklin Park Zoo much earlier than the school bus. He watched through binoculars as his son exited the bus. He saw how excited he was and wanted to grab him and tell him that *he* was his father, not Jamal. He did what Tianna asked and decided to wait, but he didn't want to wait to see his son. He needed to be near him.

He watched his son jumping, running, and smiling. He was so excited about being able to see the zoo animals. He saw his teacher trying to control him, but she wasn't able to. It was like he had a sugar rush, he was so excited. Jackson couldn't wait to get near him and let him exhaust all his energy on the basketball court.

He saw each child exit the school bus and enter the gates of the zoo. He got out of his car after they entered to make sure that he wasn't recognized in case Tianna showed up at the zoo, too. He walked to the entrance to purchase a ticket. He gave the cashier his debit card and she swiped it with a smile. "Enjoy your day," was the last message he heard before he entered the gates in search of his son.

Tianna's phone rang and it was Ms. Woods on the line telling her not to panic, but her son was missing and the police had been called.

"What do you mean my son is missing?!"

Ms. Woods explained how they were at the zoo and Ms. Kathy let a man take Tyler because she thought he was a chaperone, but now they were unable to locate them. Tianna hung up the phone in a frenzy and then she, Michelle, and X were on their way to the zoo.

She called Jackson on her way and he answered after the second ring.

"Jackson, our son is missing," she said in a panic.

"Calm down. I'm at the zoo and I will find him. I just saw him walk inside the gates a little while ago."

"Are you sure? Ms. Woods called and said that they can't find him. We are on our way to the zoo right now."

Tianna hung up and thought about calling Jamal but knew that he may be in rehab, so she decided to wait to call him and try to find Tyler without worrying him.

She didn't get a chance to ask Jackson what he was doing at the zoo.

It wasn't important. She wanted him to find her son!

"How do you know my mommy? And this is not the way to my mommy's house," Tyler said while riding in the back seat of the car. Mark White didn't say a word. He kept speeding down the dirt roads to his home to teach Tianna a lesson about cheating and having a child behind his back.

"Where are we going?" Tyler continued to ask.

"Shut up!" Mark yelled.

"I want my mommy and daddy!" Tyler cried.

Hearing Tyler say "mommy and daddy" in a sentence made Mark livid. He clinched the steering wheel tight as he continued driving over the speed limit. He didn't look like the Mark he was before he went to prison, a clean-cut college white boy, instead, he looked disheveled and had a full beard and his hair was shaved bald.

Tyler continued to cry for Tianna and Jamal, but Mark turned up the radio to muffle his cries.

What he didn't notice was a car following behind him.

Mark pulled into his driveway and told Tyler to stop his crying before he gave him something to cry about. He put the child locks on Tyler's door so that he couldn't get out. He threatened Tyler not to move before he went inside his home.

A quiet knock could be heard on Tyler's window and a man stood there with his finger up to his lips telling Tyler to be quiet.

Tyler immediately stopped crying.

The man opened the door and told Tyler that it was going to be okay. He picked Tyler up and took him to his car. He locked him inside and told him that he would be right back.

"Who are you?" Tyler asked.

"I'm your fa—" Jackson started to say. "I'm Jackson and don't worry. I got you. I'm going to lock you inside, just don't get out. Okay?"

"Okay," Tyler said as he wiped away his tears.

Jackson walked up to Mark's front door and grabbed a brick that was lying on the ground. He waited outside the door until Mark came outside.

There were sirens in the distance because Jackson called Tianna as he saw Mark leaving the zoo with Tyler. She'd notified the police and knew exactly where Mark lived.

When Mark opened the front door, he had a shovel, tape, and a rope. He closed and locked the door. As soon as he turned around he was met with the brick upside his forehead. Jackson then hovered over him, beating Mark into oblivion with his fists.

"Don't you ever come around my family again, you motherfucker! I will kill you!" Jackson repeated even though Mark was knocked unconscious from the first punch.

"Sir, stand back and put your hands up!"

Jackson continued beating Mark unaware that the police were there.

"Sir, put your hands up! Before I shoot!"

Tianna, Michelle, and X drove up and got out of the car.

Jackson stopped and put his hands up He did what Officer Bryant told him. He began walking toward Jackson reminding him not to move and keep his hands up where he could see them. He told Jackson to put his hands behind his back. And within seconds, even though Jackson did what he was told, he was thrown to the ground and handcuffed.

"Officer, no, he's not the one that kidnapped my son! He's the father," Tianna cried.

"Tianna, just go to the car and get my son. He's in the back seat," Jackson said.

Tianna went to get Tyler out of Jackson's car and took him to X's car so that he wouldn't see what was happening. She kept asking Tyler if he was okay and did Mark hurt him? Tyler said no but he was scared.

"Shut up! You are under arrest. You have the right to remain silent. Anything you say can and will be used against you," Officer, Bryant said as he read Jackson his rights and escorted him to the police car.

"Officer, you have the wrong man! He's not the kidnapper."
Michelle continued to say, but to no avail.

X then jumped in and asked the officer why he was arresting the
wrong man. The officer told X to stand back or else he will be going to
jail for interfering with a peace officer.

"I know my rights. I 'm not interfering with anything. You are
arresting an innocent Black man!" X retorted.

The ambulance arrived and two EMT's pulled out a stretcher and placed
Mark on it and rushed him inside the truck. They took his vitals and
examined his wounds. He was still alive and breathing, but unconscious.
Mark was taken to the nearest hospital and Jackson was taken to the jail.

Chapter Ten

Michelle and X followed the cruiser to the police department while Tianna and Tyler got into another ambulance to go to the hospital to get Tyler examined. She cried and hugged him tight while looking him over for any injuries. They arrived at the hospital and Tyler was examined and questioned by the police officer. They were released after two hours.

"Those racist pigs arrested Jackson simply because of his skin color. They didn't want to hear who the real kidnapper was. I can't stand them motherfuckers. 'Serve and protect,' my ass."

"X, I know how you feel but we can't go down there with an attitude. Let's go and explain the situation. And leave peacefully."

"You're right, but this is the type of thing that I constantly protest against. It makes me upset that we continue to be profiled because of the color of our skin."

"Please, let's not make it worse."

Michelle and X entered the police station and walked to the desk to get information on Jackson Norwood. The officer told him that he was in the back for questioning.

"What is he being charged with, Officer Reynolds?" X asked.

"He's not being charged with anything. He is being interrogated about the kidnapping.

"Officer, Jackson Norwood was not the kidnapper. Mark White, who was released from prison, is the kidnapper. He took Tyler and Jackson is his father. He rescued his son," Michelle explained.

Officer Reynolds called to the back to speak with the officers that were interrogating Jackson, and told them what Michelle said. She was allowed to go into the room with Jackson and explain everything. Chief Wilson said they wouldn't be hearing from Mark White again. As soon as he was released from the hospital he would be returning to prison for a very long time. After the statements were made and each one sworn in, an hour later, Jackson was released.

Tianna, Michelle, and X sat in the living room talking about the kidnapping and the charges Mark would be facing once he was transported back to prison. Tianna would finally be at ease knowing that she wouldn't see Mark ever again. And that he couldn't hurt her or her son.

They talked about the kidnapping because it was all over the local news. Tianna turned the TV off and they talked for about an hour until Michelle decided to ask about Jackson and Jamal, two men that were madly in love with Tianna. Michelle wanted to know two things, and two things only. When was Tianna going to tell Jamal about Jackson, but most importantly when will she tell Tyler about Jackson?

"I sure wouldn't want to be in your shoes," Michelle said.

"If my opinion is warranted," X said. "I think you should be honest and up front with both men. Jamal is a cool dude and he has been down with you since day one. Even though Jackson is the father, he still left you when you needed him the most."

"In Jackson's defense, he's not responsible for Mark's actions. He had no idea he was a woman beater. Besides, he sure beat his ass and I think it had to do with the kidnapping of his son *and* the attack against you," Michelle retorted as she placed her MacBook Pro on the coffee table to pay more attention to the conversation.

"Where is Jackson?" X asked.

"He should be over later tonight. He is making plans to move here to be closer to his son. He wants to tell Tyler tonight about him being his father, but I don't think it's a good idea or the right time."

"Tianna there is never a good time with you. You should have been up front from the beginning. The man has missed four years of his son's life and you want him to miss more?" Michelle said.

"No, I just don't want to hurt anyone."

"It's a little too late for that," X said as he got up to answer the doorbell.

Jamal stood at the door on crutches. He had good news to tell Tianna and his son. He didn't suffer a torn ACL as the sports analyst predicted. He had a severe ankle sprain and would be out for three to six weeks rehabbing. He planned to rehab in Boston so that he could be closer to his son.

Tianna overheard Jamal talking. She didn't know what she was going to do with Jamal *and* Jackson in Boston. She didn't want to tell him that she and Jackson were engaged again.

She loved Jamal but she couldn't tell her heart to love him the way she loved Jackson. She'd tried for years.

Jamal took care of her and Tyler. He gave her a ten-thousand-dollar-a-month allowance. He was the perfect father to Tyler. She couldn't ask for anything more from him. He gave her his all.

She believed in Jamal more than Jackson. She entrusted all her secrets to Jamal. She knew that he would always be by her side no matter what. He truly loved all of her.

So why wasn't she engaged to Jamal instead of Jackson? Jackson had something that Jamal could never have, and it was that Jackson was her first. The first to take her virginity and the one she bore her only son with. The first to capture her heart.

"Daddy! Are you okay?" Tyler asked as he ran down the stairs to greet and hug Jamal.

"Hey son, yeah, Daddy is fine."

"Why aren't you at school?"

"A man kidnapped me from the zoo yesterday and Jackson saved me."

Jamal looked at Tianna and wondered why she didn't tell him about the kidnapping. He also wanted to know which Jackson? He prayed that it wasn't Jackson Norwood, and if so, what was he doing in Boston?

"Hey, Jamal," Tianna said as she walked up to hug him.

"What's going on?" he asked.

"Oh yeah, I was going to call you and tell you, but I knew that you were rehabbing and I didn't want to bother you," she tried to explain before he cut her off.

"I don't care what I'm doing, when it involves my son, please call me."

Michelle and X excused themselves to give Jamal and Tianna some privacy.

She helped him get comfortable on the sofa and prop his ankle up.

"Daddy, when are you going to be able to play basketball again?"

"Soon, son, soon."

"Sweetie, do you want to go in your room and play with your toys so that I can talk to your dad in private?"

"What's does *private* mean?"

"It means that I need to speak to Daddy alone."

"Ut oh, did I say something wrong?"

"No, sweetie, you didn't say anything wrong. Your dad and I have to discuss something very important."

"Let daddy talk to mommy and then I will come and play with you, okay?" Jamal said.

"Yayyy, can we play Mortal Kombat?"

"No!" Tianna and Jamal said in unison.

Tyler had always tried to get them to let him play Mortal Kombat but it was not age appropriate.

As soon as Tyler left for his room, Tianna began singing like a canary and told Jamal about the kidnapping and Jackson. Jamal was grateful that Jackson saved his son and that Mark didn't hurt him, but wanted to know what Jackson was doing in Boston.

"Jackson knows about Tyler."

"How is that? Did you tell him?"

"No. Remember when Tasha was in town and she brushed Tyler's teeth? She took the toothbrush to have a DNA test done. The test showed that Tyler was her nephew. She gave Jackson the results of the test."

Jamal couldn't believe it. He put his head down and rubbed the top of it and blew out a sigh. He was not ready to give up Tianna or Tyler, but both could be gone now that Jackson knew the truth. He'd known that the secret wouldn't last forever but he was hoping it would last until Tianna gave her heart to him. By then, it wouldn't matter whether Jackson knew about Tyler because he would securely have them both.

"Does Tyler know?"

"No, he doesn't."

"When are you going to tell him?"

"I don't know."

"Let me tell him," Jamal said as a tear ran down his face.

"Are you sure?"

"Yeah, I love my little man and I want him to know that, even though my blood doesn't run through his veins. I would give my life for him."

Jamal wiped his tears and pulled himself up off the sofa to walk to Tyler's room. Tianna tried to help him, but he had too much pride to let her. He did everything for himself. He didn't ask her how she got the hickey on the left side of her neck. He already knew who and where it came from as soon as he heard the name, Jackson. No matter how disappointed he was, he still and would always love her.

Tianna turned the TV back on and sat on the sofa and watched the local news plaster the kidnapping on all stations. She was glad that Jamal didn't see the local news before he arrived in town so she could tell him.

A soft knock could be heard at Tyler's bedroom door. He sat on his bed watching *Paw Patrol*. Tyler begged his mother for a puppy, but she refused to get one because she didn't have time to take care of it.

"Who is it?" Tyler asked.

Jamal didn't answer because he didn't know how since he was there to talk to Tyler about his biological father. So he said nothing. He wanted to say "Daddy," but how could he? He opened the door, hobbled in, and sat on the bed. He dried his tears as much as he could without Tyler being suspicious. He rested his crutches against Tyler's chair that sat under the computer desk.

Tyler noticed the scowl on Jamal's face but didn't know if it was from his sprained ankle.

"Are you okay, Daddy?"

Jamal couldn't resist. Hearing Tyler call him daddy meant so much. It was one of his greatest gifts. He put his head down and cried into the palm of his hands.

"What's wrong, Daddy?" Tyler asked as he began to cry, seeing his father in distress.

He gave Jamal a hug and stood between his legs trying to remove his hands from his face to see if Jamal was crying. Jamal wouldn't remove his hands because he didn't want Tyler to see him.

"Are you crying?"

"Naw, son. My ankle is in a little bit of pain, but I'm going to be all right. You know Daddy loves you, right?"

"I know. I love you, too."

The words were not coming out the way Jamal planned before he walked upstairs. He knew it would be difficult, but he didn't realize how he was going to tell Tyler.

So, Tyler began telling Jamal what he came to tell him.

"I know you are here to tell me the man that rescued me is my daddy."

Jamal looked up and said in disbelief, "You're too smart for your own good."

Tyler overheard his mother, X, and Michelle talking the night of the kidnapping and he heard Tianna and Jamal talking before he came into the room. He was already prepared. But he was still too young to understand the significance of Jamal not being his father or the seriousness of the kidnapping.

"Are you still going to come see me and take me places?"

"Absolutely. I would never leave you. You will always be my son, that's right here." Jamal said as he patted the left side of his chest, meaning his heart.

Tyler placed his head on Jamal's chest and just sat there listening to Jamal's heartbeat. Jamal hugged him tight and didn't want to let go. He asked Tyler if the kidnapper harmed him and Tyler said no. Jamal was hurt that he wasn't there to protect him.

Tyler had one question and one question only.

Tianna stood outside the doorway watching their embrace and hearing Tyler ask the million-dollar question.

"Can I still call you Daddy?"

Chapter Eleven

Spring break and it was time to travel home to Texas and
introduce Tyler to his grandparents. He had already met Tianna's side of
the family years ago but now it was time to meet the Norwoods.

Tyler was so excited and couldn't wait. He was introduced to
Jackson as his father a few weeks earlier and they had been spending
time together before Jackson left to go back home. He knew that Tyler
and Tianna would be down within a week. He missed them both and
couldn't wait to pick them up at the airport.

"Mama, how far away is Texas?" Tyler asked.

"It's almost two thousand miles."

"Wow, that's a lonnnnng way. Is it this long?" Tyler opened his
arms as wide as he could to demonstrate the distance between Texas and
Massachusetts.

"No, it's this far." Tianna demonstrated with a round globe that
sat on the desk in the study.

Tianna's phone rang and it was Tasha. She knew that Tianna and
Tyler were arriving later that night and wanted to welcome them. She
wanted to offer her home to them, but Tianna declined and let her know
that they would be staying with her mother. Besides, she wasn't too
happy about Tasha going behind her back and getting a DNA sample
from her son. She knew she was in the wrong to hide Tyler from his real
father, but she wanted to disclose the truth in her own time, not Tasha's.

"Hey, Tasha."

"Hey, T, I can't wait to see you and my nephew."

Tianna's phone beeped and she put Tasha on hold.

"Hello?"

Tianna could only hear breathing and the sound of a honking horn
and morning traffic in the background.

"Hello?" she repeated, but there was no answer or number on the
caller ID.

"Don't call this phone again," Tianna said and clicked over to
speak with Tasha.

"Who was that on the other line?" Tasha asked.

"No one. They didn't say anything. I've been getting these weird calls lately."

"Are you sure it isn't Mark's crazy ass?"

"I'm sure. He's going to rot in prison for what he did," Tianna assured Tasha.

"I hope so. I was just calling to see if you wanted me to pick you and Tyler up from the airport."

"Jackson is picking us up."

"Oh okay. Well, I will see you soon."

Tianna ended the call and she noticed Michelle coming from the kitchen in a somber mood. She didn't have family in town and came from a broken home. She acquired a full scholarship to Harvard.

Tianna asked her several times if she wanted to travel with her and Tyler, but she felt that she would be in the way of family time. Tianna assured her she wouldn't be. Michelle had always been there for her ever since they'd met freshman year. She confided in her, they confided in each other. She considered Michelle like a sister. And Tianna didn't want her spending spring break alone.

"Michelle, are you sure you don't want to come with us?"

"Girl, how many times are you going to ask me that?"

"Until you tell me that you are going!"

"Well, I'm not. I'm going to stick around and attend some of X's *revolutionary* rallies." She laughed.

Tianna admired X and knew that he was going to change the world one day. He was that knowledgeable and persistent about social equality for Black Americans, who he called, *American Aborigines*. Meaning Black people were indigenous to the Americas and didn't come from Africa on a slave boat.

"Why y'all down here talking about me on the cool?" X interrupted coming from his bedroom.

"Ain't nobody talking about you. What time is your rally?" Michelle asked.

"It begins at seven p.m. but I need some help setting things up. Are you down with helping me?"

"Anything for you, Malcolm X," Michelle said as she playfully kissed him on his cheek.

"I think she likes me," X joked.

"In your dreams," Michelle hissed.

"Yeah, I know you be dreaming about me, that's why I can't get any sleep at night. They say if you can't sleep it's because someone is thinking about you."

"Anywhoo, I'm going to drop Tianna and Tyler at the airport and then I'll be on my way."

"Thank you. I appreciate you."

"You better," Michelle retorted as she headed upstairs.

"We must strive for greatness like our forefathers. How many of you have ever heard about the first airplane attack in America on a small district called Greenwood in Tulsa, Oklahoma?"

The crowd was silent. X talked about Black Wall Street and the destruction of Black owned businesses and homes.

"History deems Black Wall Street as a riot."

Michelle listened in, admiring X and how he told the story that had been hidden from the history books. She had never heard of Black Wall Street until she met X. She wished Tianna was there to hear him speak. It was one of his greatest appearances.

She'd dropped Tianna and Tyler off at the airport over an hour ago and now she was watching her friend speak.

Malcolm continued, "I'm here to tell you that it was a genocide against Black Americans and the establishments that they worked hard to create during the Jim Crow era of segregation. Riot my ass, it was a genocide! Our people owned schools, hospitals, movie theaters. Many types of businesses as you can imagine, they owned them all. Most importantly, the Black dollar stayed in the community for over a year.

The citizens of Greenwood, Oklahoma understood the value of the dollar and how important it was to unify and do for ourselves."

"Yeah, that's right. We need to get back to group economics," a male undergraduate student yelled from the crowd.

X heard the comment and agreed with the student. He talked about how Black people can unify and put their money together in a saving account. Each Black person in America could contribute five dollars a month to a savings account and the money would be spent creating Black owned businesses all over the world like Black Wall Street. He kept saying how much spending power the Black community had but that they were unorganized.

He talked about how Black people's identities were stripped away from them when the colonizers came and destroyed their land in 1492. How they destroyed the land in Tulsa, Oklahoma in 1921.

"We are Aborigines. We didn't come from Africa. Well, some of us did, but 95% of Black Americans were already in America when Christopher Columbus discovered our ancestors."

X spoke and answered questions for over two hours. He had all night and day to talk about a Black revolution. He talked about harvesting crops and buying land to cultivate.

He handed out pamphlets and his contact information for those who were willing to take a stand in rebuilding Black Wall Street, making it more iron clad than before.

Malcolm X wanted leaders and warriors. He had a plan to move the Black communities forward in society.

After the rally ended, Michelle was in awe about how many people were interested in X's plan. There were about fifty people that left their email addresses and phone numbers to continue to collaborate and organize. Most of them were men.

Michelle walked up to X and said, "You know you are wasting your time, right?"

"What you mean?"

"Your ass should be preparing for the presidency because you could run for President of the United States of America. And you got my vote!"

He hugged her and laughed. He'd never thought about running for president but the race for a senate seat was in his near future.

Chapter Twelve

 Tianna and Tyler arrived at San Antonio International Airport.

The building was crowded with people flying in and out for spring break.
There was a military husband running toward his wife and son crying in
each other's arms. It looked like he just got back from a tour of duty in
the Afghanistan War.

"Mommy, where is Jackson?"
Tyler still hadn't gotten around to calling Jackson "dad" or
"daddy." Jamal still owned that title. Jackson understood though, he
knew that his son had to get to know him better before he became
"Daddy."
"He should be here. Let me call him to see where he's at."
Tianna pulled her cell phone from her purse to dial Jackson's number, but
she received his voicemail. She left several messages but no call back
after waiting almost an hour after they arrived. Tyler was getting grumpy
and they both felt the jet lag.
She didn't know whether to call Tasha or Jamal. She didn't want
to disturb Jamal since he was still rehabbing his ankle. It was too late to
call Tasha and she didn't want to wake her. Bernadette was at work.
She'd spoken to her the night before letting her know that she and Tyler
would be there around midnight. So, she called an Uber.
They arrived at her mother's home thirty minutes later. The Uber
driver was courteous enough to assist Tianna with her luggage. She
tipped him very well.
She unlocked the front door and disarmed the alarm. Everything
was the same as she'd left it years ago. Except her mother had bought
new furniture and remodeled the kitchen.
She and Tyler were as quiet as possible because she didn't want
to awake her grandmother. But before they could reach the stairs,
Grandma Debby turned the light on.
"I know you ain't sneaking in here without me seeing you and my
great grandbaby."

"Ohhh Granny, I didn't want to wake you. I know you have work in the morning."

"I don't care nothing about no work. I want to see my grandbabies."

Debby grabbed Tyler, squeezed him tight, and left kisses all over him. She tried to pick him up but her bad back wouldn't let her. Tyler was so elated being embraced by her love and attention. He barely remembered her because it had been a little over a year since the last time he'd seen her.

"Let me look at my great grandbaby. You're so handsome. He looks just like Jackson, though, not Jamal."

"Granny, I know. Tyler and everyone know the truth. Jackson is Tyler's father."

"I knew it. I just wanted you to come clean. That boy has always loved you."

"Can we talk about this tomorrow? I'm tired and I have to give Tyler a bath."

"Sure, baby. I will see you in the morning or after work."
Tianna and Tyler went to her old room to shower and get some sleep. She didn't call Jackson and decided to wait until morning to see why he didn't pick them up from the airport.

Roxanne began undressing Jackson. She took off his shoes, followed by his socks, and worked herself upward until he was stark naked. She took out her cell phone and began taking pictures and posting them to her Facebook account. Jackson was unresponsive as she took selfies of her naked body lying alongside of him in his bed.

Earlier in the day when they were at work, Jackson had informed Roxanne that they wouldn't be able to see each other because he was engaged and had a child. She was distraught but kept her cool and told him that she needed to speak with him in private about something real important. She offered to meet at his house later and he reluctantly obliged.

When she arrived at his home, she had tears in her eyes, holding the results of a home pregnancy test in her hand. Jackson welcomed her in, and they took a seat on the sofa. She told him that she was two months pregnant and that he was going to be a father. She knew he was engaged but didn't know what to do.

Jackson couldn't believe it, so he went into the kitchen to fix himself a drink. He sat the drink down and went into his room to check his phone to see if Tianna had called since she was due at the airport within an hour.

During the time he was gone, Roxanne put a liquid in his drink and stirred it with a tongue depressor. She placed the tongue depressor back in her coat pocket along with the liquid. Jackson came back into the living room and Roxanne begin to cry even more. He couldn't stand to see her cry, but he didn't love Roxanne and couldn't see himself having a child with her. She was a fling, something to do to get over Tianna, and she wasn't even his girl.

He grabbed his drink and chugged it down in one shot. He came closer to her to try and comfort her. Thinking about what he was going to do. He wasn't a man to abandon his responsibility, but his life was with Tianna and Tyler, not Roxanne and her unborn child.

He walked to the kitchen to pour himself another drink. He sat down and noticed that he began to feel dizzy. He could hear Roxanne speaking but couldn't understand what she was saying. He could see two of her and his head started to spin. Roxanne stopped crying and quickly disposed of the GHB, the date-rape drug. She assisted Jackson into his bedroom before he completely passed out.

She heard his cell phone ring and Tianna and Tyler's picture appeared with text that read, "My Hearts," with emojis next to it. She saw that Tianna left a message.

The phone rang three more times at five minutes apart. Jackson lay naked in his bed. Roxanne continued her photo shoot with a sinister grin.

She took pictures of her flat tummy and labeled it, "Jackson Jr."

She got all kinds of likes and comments within minutes of her Facebook posting.

She didn't respond to anyone. She just kept posting.

Chapter Thirteen

Tianna and Tyler sat at the table eating breakfast when
Bernadette got home from her overnight shift at the hospital. She was
ecstatic to see her grandbaby and daughter. She sat at the table and talked
them to death. She kissed Tyler and left lipstick all over him before she
went to her room to get some sleep. She only needed a few hours she told
them and then they could go around town because she was off for the
next three days.

Tianna asked her mother if she could borrow her car to go check
on Jackson because he didn't pick them up at the airport and wasn't
answering his phone. Since Jackson was Tyler's father, Bernadette didn't
object, but she wasn't happy hearing that her daughter and grandson were
stood up. And she was a little concerned as to why. She handed Tianna
the keys and told her to be careful.

Tianna and Tyler got into the car. She stopped at the Norwood
home first to introduce them to their grandchild. She was disappointed
that Jackson wasn't there to see his parents' faces when they saw Tyler
for the first time.

"Oh, he looks just like his father when he was a baby," Sharon
cooed like a child.

"Yeah, he certainly is the spitting image of Jackson," Adonis
agreed.

"Where is Jackson?" Tasha asked as she walked into the house
unannounced.

"Hey Tasha," Tianna said as she hugged her friend.

"What are you doing here?" Sharon asked.

"I can't come by and see my parents?"

"Yes, baby, anytime," Adonis said as he kissed his daughter.

"Hi Tyler, look at you, looking so handsome." Tasha said.

Tyler smiled big and gave Tasha a hug. She smothered him with
kisses just like both of his grandmothers. He inherited a family that was
full of love. He was one lucky little boy.

Sharon discussed how she was going to make Tyler his own room for when he visited her and could stay with them for the summer. Their first grandchild was going to be spoiled rotten.

Tianna wanted to go check on Jackson since she hadn't heard from him and asked if Tyler could stay with them until she got back. The Norwoods were elated to spend quality time with their grandchild and even said that he could spend the night. Tianna wasn't sure about him spending the night since she and her mother and Tyler were supposed to go out today.

"I could bring him by tomorrow and let him spend the night," Tianna suggested.

The Norwoods were happy to see their grandbaby, so any time with him was appreciated.

"Tasha, can you take me to Jackson's house?"

"Girl, you don't even have to ask. Let's go."

Tianna and Tasha got into Bernadette's car and were on their way to Borne Road.

Tianna explained to Tasha how she hadn't heard from Jackson all night and how he stood them up at the airport. How she called and left messages but still had no response. Tasha agreed with Tianna that it wasn't like him and was concerned about her brother.

Tasha dialed his number while on their way and got his voicemail but it was full so she wasn't able to leave a message.

As they pulled up to the house, they saw Roxanne leaving wearing a trench coat as she put her hair into a ponytail. She got in her red Porsche and sped off. She didn't see Tasha and Tianna, but they saw her.

"Oh no she didn't just come from my brother's house."

"Who is she?" Tianna asked.

"She works with Jackson; I don't know her name. Thankfully, I have a key to his house."

Tianna pulled into the driveway and killed the car engine. She and Tasha got out of the car. Tasha grabbed the newspaper from the front lawn. She knocked on the door and rang her brother's doorbell and called his name, but no answer.

She opened her Michael Kors purse to retrieve the house key, unlocked the door, and she and Tianna walked into his immaculate bachelor-decor home. Jackson had very little furniture and there was lots of space between each piece.

They walked into the kitchen area and then the living room, calling his name as they crept through the house. They walked upstairs to his bedroom, opened the door, and Jackson was lying naked in his bed sound asleep with the alarm buzzing. Lying next to him were pictures of Roxanne and Jackson.

Tianna picked up one of the pictures and began to cry. She threw the picture back on the bed.

"Jackson, Jackson, wake up," Tasha said as she shook him out of his deep sleep.

He opened his eyes half-way and was too incoherent to understand what Tasha was saying. She was just as distraught as Tianna. She'd never seen her brother in this position before.

She went into the restroom to grab his robe to cover him. He was trying to talk, but his head was pounding, and he felt drunk even though he only had *one* drink.

Tianna just stood there in disbelief looking at all the pics of her man with another woman. Not only her man but her fiancé. She stood there with her hand over her mouth with tears running down her face. She wanted to get out of there and fast.

Jackson tried to stand and go to the restroom. He kept gagging like he needed to vomit.

"Jackson, what is wrong with you?" Tasha cried.

He tried to speak but couldn't. Tasha immediately ran to the kitchen to get him a glass of water. She also got a bucket of cold water to pour on him. When that didn't work, she told Tianna to give her a hand so that she could take him to the emergency room.

Tianna kept opening his dresser draw searching for underwear, but Tasha told her to forget the underwear and grab some pants and a shirt. She did what she was told.

They both began putting his pants on and finally his shirt. Tianna found some house slippers and tried to put them on his feet. One slipper kept falling off.

"Tianna, just forget about the slippers and let's get him to the car!"

They each grabbed an arm and wrapped them around their necks. His big arms hung heavy over their small physiques. Jackson kept mumbling and squinting his eyes. He gagged a few more times before throwing up all over his doorway. He kept mumbling incoherently. Tasha locked the front door and they were on their way to University Hospital.

While in the car, he threw up again. The more he threw up, his speech became clearer.

"Tianna, I'm sorry, baby," Jackson kept saying.

Tianna said nothing. She kept driving and looking ahead. She was more concerned about her soon to be *ex-fiancé* messing up Bernadette's car.

"Tasha, don't tell Mama," he mumbled.

"Jackson, I'm not. I'm more concerned about getting you to the hospital to see what is wrong with you."

"I had one drink while Roxanne was at my house."

"We saw a white girl leaving when we pulled up. Is that Roxanne?" Tasha asked.

Jackson didn't respond. He just laid back in the seat trying not to throw up again.

They pulled up to the emergency room doors. Patients on stretchers were being wheeled in and an ambulance was out front. Tianna parked behind the ambulance.

Jackson was able to walk better than before, so Tianna and Tasha's necks and shoulders caught a break. He kept telling Tianna how sorry he was and begging Tasha not to call their parents. To keep this between the two of them. He also asked about his underwear.
Tasha promised that she wouldn't say anything. She told him that they couldn't find his underwear.

They walked up to the nurse's desk to be seen as urgent care. Tasha described all the symptoms Jackson was having. The nurse asked for his medical insurance, but he didn't have his wallet with him. He was able to give the name of his healthcare provider but that was it.

Tasha offered to pay cash, but needed someone to see her brother, now. The nurse gave Tasha the paperwork to fill out. She gave it to Tianna to complete. She couldn't think because of the concern for her brother.

"I have to go move the car. I'll be right back." She would get to the paperwork when she returned. Tianna parked the car and retrieved a parking ticket. She rushed back to the emergency room.

Tianna filled out the paperwork as best she could while the nurse, Tasha, and Jackson walked into the back of the emergency room.

Nurse Williams took his vitals and began questioning him. Jackson said that he had a friend at his home, and he had one drink, and after the drink is when he began to get dizzy.

Ms. Williams asked what type of drink and if he left his drink alone with his friend in his home. He admitted that he had.

"Oh my God, she better not have poisoned my brother!" Tasha cried.

"Where's my fiancé?" Jackson kept calling for Tianna.

"Where's my underwear?"

"Jackson, I already told you that we couldn't find your underwear."

"Tasha, you got me in here with my ass out and no underwear? My balls are all over the place."

"Boy, nobody can see your ass. And I'm sorry about your testicles." Tasha laughed.

While Tianna finished with the paperwork, she walked to the other end of the nurse's station to give them the information and to get buzzed inside the double doors to check on Jackson.

"Excuse me Ms.," Tianna said.

The nurse turned around and they both were shocked looking at each other.

"Shantae?"

"Yes, it's me," Shantae said. She wanted to say, "Tar Baby," but she had matured since high school. She graduated from nursing school as a registered nurse and acquired her bachelor's in nursing at the University of Incarnate Word.

She married the Lebron James look-alike who she cheated on Jackson with.

"Tianna, how have you been?"

"I've been good. I'm here with Jackson and Tasha. Jackson is very ill and we don't know what's wrong with him," Tianna said with concern.

"Where is he?"

"He's in the back being checked in. I wanted to know if I could go back there with him?"

"Sure, let me buzz you in and see what's going on with him."

"Thanks, Shantae. I really appreciate it."

"No problem. I owe you anyway."

"For what?"

"Being so mean to you growing up," she said in a sincere tone.

"We are grown now, so your apology is accepted." Tianna smiled. She didn't know whether to hug Shantae because she didn't want to be embarrassed if she didn't return the embrace. So, she waited for Shantae to buzz her in and they both walked to the back of the emergency unit to find Jackson.

Shantae checked each chart on the outsides of the doors. She located Jackson in Room #3 and knocked on the door before entering. Ms. Williams could be heard talking to Jackson, so neither heard the timid knock on the door.

Shantae called out to Ms. Williams as she and Tianna made their entrance.

Tasha was the first to see Shantae,

"What are you doing here?" she asked.

"Hey, I know you. You're my cheating ex-girlfriend."

"Nice to see you, Tasha and Jackson."

"Get her out of here," Jackson said.

"Jackson, be nice. We are no longer in high school. Shantae is a nurse and she works here. She helped me find you."

"Well, I will let Ms. Williams take it from here," Shantae said as she made her exit.

"Good idea," Tasha hissed.

"It was good seeing you, Tianna."

"Likewise," Tianna said.

"Oh, so now, she's *Tianna*? And not Tar Baby?" Jackson yelled as Shantae left the room. She continued walking as though she didn't hear him.

She got outside the door and a tear fell from her eye. She knew she deserved what just happened, but she was not the same Shantae she was in high school. She felt bad about how she treated Tianna and Jackson. She wanted to apologize to Jackson, but she thought another time at another place would be best. He still resented her, but she still had love for him. She wished she could have a do-over.

Shantae couldn't help but notice the engagement ring on Tianna's finger. She wanted to ask if it was from Jackson, but didn't want to hear that it was.

She'd seen Darren at a local Mom and Pop store a year ago and pretended not to see him. She heard that he and Tasha were married and she saw his ring to confirm it. She also knew that Jackson didn't make it to the NBA and graduated from pharmacy school.

"Jackson, we are going to run some tests on you," nurse Williams said.

She asked that Tianna and Tasha wait out in the waiting room. Jackson reluctantly obliged with the nurse's orders; he didn't want Tianna to go anywhere. He knew that she was upset with him but didn't know she saw naked pictures of him and Roxanne. He hadn't seen the pictures himself.

He tried giving Tianna a kiss, but she turned away. She wanted him to get better and it looked as if he was starting to regain his speech and memory. Throwing up caused him to recover faster.

Tianna and Tasha walked to the waiting room. They had to pass Shantae on their way out. She smiled at them but only Tianna returned the gesture. Tasha wanted nothing to do with Shantae of old or Shantae of new. She had done too much to ever get into her good graces.

"Can you believe that heifer?" Tasha hissed as she and Tianna sat down in the hard-plastic chairs in the waiting room filled with cranky children and family waiting for their sick relatives.

"Tasha, just let it go. We are not teenagers anymore."

"Yeah, but we are not too far removed, and I still want to kick her ass."

"It's not worth it. Besides, I'm worried about Jackson, not Shantae."

Tianna was right, so Tasha got back on the subject of her brother. She suspected that Roxanne put some kind of chemical in her brother's drink. She told Tianna that she saw Roxanne at her brother's job one day when she came to visit him, but she didn't think Jackson had a thing for white girls. And couldn't believe those naked pictures that were left on his bed.

"I know my brother didn't sleep with her, T."

"How do you know?" Tianna asked as she rolled her eyes.

"My brother has never been into nothing but Black women. Unlike you. You seem to have forgotten about your *little* Mark."

"Tash, that's different." Tianna said as she shifted back in her seat to try and explain.

"How so? They both are white."

Tianna explained how she met Mark when she was vulnerable and at a very low point in her life. She talked about how she wanted to commit suicide because she felt that Tasha being in the accident and in a coma was her fault. She'd almost killed her best friend. She was in love with Jackson but couldn't let her feelings be known because of it. She didn't want to lose Tasha as a friend.
And she was suffering from subconscious self-hate from being called derogatory names all her life.
Mark made her feel special. She was lonely and needed a friend. He embraced her as a friend and gave her the attention she needed. But he had a dark side.

"I told you not to play with those white dolls when we were growin' up. Why you think we always bought you Black dolls?"

"Tasha, this isn't about no baby dolls," Tianna hissed.

"Yes, it is, because you were idolizing those white dolls instead of being comfortable in your own skin. Those dolls mess with your subconscious. **All Black little girls need to play with dolls that look like them.**"

Tianna admitted that she never thought about why the Norwoods always bought her Black dolls. She would play with the white dolls the most and set the Black ones aside or put them in the closet. She preferred the white *pretty* dolls.

The conversation between them was all over the place. They talked about everything. But the talks were getting too deep and before Tianna let it slip her mind again, she asked Tasha about brushing Tyler's teeth and getting his DNA examined.

"Why did you go behind my back and take a sample of Tyler's DNA?"

"Because I knew that you and my brother had secretly been seeing each other. I saw you kissing on Christmas day in the car when he gave you a necklace."

Tianna gasped because she was busted. Tasha went on to explain how she calculated the months and when she came to visit her on spring break that she looked pregnant.

Tasha knew she was pregnant even before Tianna knew.

When Tasha saw Tyler, she was immediately attached to him. And was amazed at how much he looked like her brother.

Tianna had never been a good liar and Tasha read her like a book. She knew Tyler was her nephew. She wanted to make Tyler official and see him raised in a two-parent household. She also wanted to be an auntie.

"So, when are you and Jackson getting married?"

"We made plans for after I graduate. But I don't know."

"Do you love him?"

"What kind of question is that?"

"It's an honest one," Tasha said as she looked directly into Tianna's eyes. She raised her eyebrow and waited for an answer. Tianna thought about it and then she spoke.

"Yes, I've always loved him. He was my first." Tianna smiled inside and out thinking about her relationship with Jackson. She truly loved him. When she found out that she was pregnant, she was in shock but she and Jackson weren't just together on Christmas night. It had been the entire school break. They couldn't get enough of each other. And each time they were together they never used protection. But Tianna never thought about getting pregnant.

"What about Jamal?" Tasha asked.

Tianna didn't know why Tasha asked, but she acknowledged her love for him. How much he meant to her and the father's role he took on to cover for her. But Tasha wanted to know if she had slept with him. Tianna laughed and said,

"I don't kiss and tell." She stuck out her tongue like a five-year-old child.

They both laughed and awaited Jackson's prognosis.

An hour later, they were allowed to enter Jackson's room. The results of his blood test were back. It showed that Roxanne had spiked his drink with GHB. Tasha was furious. Tianna was upset and Jackson was concerned. He didn't know why Roxanne would do it, but most importantly, *why* she would take the risk of drugging him. What was her objective?

He thought about the results of Roxanne's pregnancy test. He was going to be a father. He didn't know how to tell Tianna or his parents. His love was for Tianna and Tyler. They were his family.

He didn't want the child with Roxanne, but what kind of man would he be asking her to get an abortion? He didn't believe in such a brutal decision. He was going to have to face reality. His father raised him to be a man with every mistake or decision he made.

Dr. Anderson entered the room to ask how Jackson was feeling and tell him that he would be released soon. He was advised to drink plenty of water.

Nurse Williams took his vitals again before he was released. They saw Shantae on the way out of the emergency room. She wished Jackson well but he said nothing and neither did Tasha. Tianna thanked her.

They walked through the exit door and got in the car. The car reeked of vomit, so they pulled into the Wash Tub to have the car cleaned before Bernadette beat everybody's ass.

"Ayye, Tash, please don't tell mom and dad about this," Jackson said.

"I already told you that I wouldn't."

"Tianna, where's my son?"

"He's at your parents' house."

Jackson wanted to see his son. He wanted to hold him in his arms. He was just grateful to be alive and that he didn't suffer any major side-effects from the drug. He didn't know whether or not to have Roxanne fired, or press charges because she was his "baby mama."

"You need to be contacting the police department to file charges on her instead of worrying about Mom and Dad."

Tianna waited to hear Jackson say that he would press charges, but he just looked out the window in deep thought.

"Jackson, did you hear what Tasha said?"

He heard her but was not going to file charges against his baby mama.

"Yeah, I will. She not getting away with it," Jackson lied. He had no intention of contacting the police. He was going to contact Roxanne to make plans for being a father but he wanted nothing to do with her. He pondered how he was going to tell his parents that he had another child on the way. What would they think of him? He didn't know how to tell Tianna that Tyler had a little sister or brother coming soon.

He hoped their love was strong enough to overcome his bad choices.

Chapter Fourteen

Tianna's cell phone rang while she was in the shower. Tyler heard the phone and answered it after the third ring. He knew who it was because he saw his daddy's picture display.

"Hi, Daddy!" Tyler was so excited to hear Jamal's voice. He'd had limited contact with Jamal since Jackson found out the truth. They weren't keeping him away from Jamal, but Tianna felt it was best for him to get to know Jackson.

"Hey, my little man. How you doing?"

"I'm fine. I miss you Daddy, are you coming to get me?"

"I don't know. Let me talk to your mom?"

"She's in the shower."

Jamal wanted to come get his son but didn't want to overstep the boundaries. He missed him. Not only him, but Tianna, too. He was no longer on crutches and knew that she was in Texas. He wanted to see her and Tyler before they left.

"Daddy, can I ask you a question?"

"Anything son, you can ask me anything."

"Is it okay if I call you 'Daddy' and Jackson 'Father'?"

Tianna heard Tyler on the phone when she was drying off and putting on her robe and knew he was talking to Jamal based on the conversation. She entered the room and got on the phone before Jamal could answer. She talked to Jamal for another five minutes. They made plans to meet before she returned to Boston.

"Mommy, wait, Daddy has to answer my question," Tyler pleaded.

Tianna put Jamal on speaker phone and said that it would be fine with her. She didn't want to confuse Tyler and didn't want to hurt Jackson or Jamal. He had only known Jamal as his dad. But to hear Tyler call Jackson a name other than father wouldn't be good. Jackson deserved to be a part of his life and build the relationship as father and son. Tianna had created the confusion and she planned to straighten it out.

"Bye, Daddy. I love you," Tyler said before they ended the call. Jamal mimicked the same sentiments. He loved Tyler and he would *always* be his son.

When Tianna hung up with Jamal, she received a phone call from Jackson inviting them to dinner at his mother's home. She agreed since she and Jackson hadn't been on good terms. They were still engaged but Tianna stayed at her mother's house to rethink the incident with Roxanne. She wanted to ask Jackson his feelings for Roxanne because she felt that there was something more between the two of them. Tianna wanted answers but didn't know if she had the right to ask since she and Jackson were not together when he was dating her. But what about the recent naked pictures of them? Did he have sex with Roxanne after they reconciled their engagement?
Did he cheat on her? She loved Jackson but she would also walk away from him if he was unfaithful.

Roxanne sat at the Longhorn Café with her twin sister Ruby. They were identical twins and you couldn't tell them apart. The only difference was Roxanne had a birthmark on her left breast. But their short blonde hair, petite figures, and hazel eyes were exactly the same. Their parents couldn't even tell them apart many times. In fact, growing up, they played acts of deception on their parents and teachers. When Ruby was on punishment, Roxanne took her place so that Ruby could go out on her dates. When Ruby was failing specific classes, Roxanne took her exams and made sure her sister passed each class. So, when Roxanne asked Ruby to go to Jackson's home and put the GHB in his drink and take pictures, it was another way of deceiving people. Something they had always done.

Ruby slid Roxanne the pics of her and Jackson. She opened the envelope and then handed her sister ten thousand dollars.

"You're the best, hun."

"I know. Toodaloo. Call you tomorrow," Ruby said as she walked out of the restaurant to catch a cab. She was on her way to Hong Kong for a new modeling gig that she was pursuing. She needed money and her sister was able to provide it for her. But for a favor.

As soon as Ruby left, Jackson entered the café looking for Roxanne. When he entered the restaurant, he bumped into Ruby going out.

"Roxanne?" He asked as he looked at her through her Ray-Ban sunglasses.

"No, I'm sorry. You have the wrong person."

Jackson blinked and shook his head. He didn't know if he was having side effects from the GHB because she looked just like Roxanne.

Roxanne saw the exchange and breathed a sigh of relief at how Ruby handled him. She got up from the table and motioned with a wave for Jackson to show where she was located. He saw her and walked toward the corner booth.

She smiled but he didn't. He was there to discuss his unborn child and talk about what she did to him. He sat down in front of her with a look of disgust plastered across his face.

He didn't waste any time getting to the point. He told her he knew about the drug she put in his drink, and the only reason he didn't have her fired or arrested was because of his unborn child. She denied putting the GHB in his drink and told him that he was hallucinating. She was repulsed that he could accuse her of such a dirty transgression. Why would she do something like that when she could have him *willingly*?

"Is that what you think, you could have me? You knew I was going back to Tianna and my son."

He told her that he didn't want anything to do with her until his child was born. He didn't want to see her around. She made him sick just sitting there being near him. He told her not to say anything to him at work, and if she did he would have her fired.

Tears began to well in her eyes and her bottom lip started to tremble, but before one tear could drop, he told her that it wasn't going to work. She could save them for the next Bozo the Clown.

He placed a one hundred dollar bill on the table, told her to make sure his child was properly nourished, and got up to walk out the restaurant.

"Jackson," she called out.

He turned around and smirked, but kept walking.

Walking out the restaurant and out of her life.

Jackson arrived at his parent's home right after his encounter with Roxanne. He had to ask his dad for advice about what to do about the situation. He didn't love her, had just found out about Tyler, and now he had another child on the way by a woman who he barely knew.

Sharon was in the kitchen preparing dinner that was almost ready. His father was in his man cave sitting in his La-Z-Boy recliner watching a Lakers game when Jackson walked in and sat in a chair next to him.

"Hey Dad, what are you up to?"

"Nothing son, what are you up to?"

"I wanted to talk to you and get your opinion about something before everyone else arrives for dinner."

His father turned away from the game and gave his son his undivided attention. He saw a look of something deeply troubling him. He knew it was something to do with Tianna.

"I got another child on the way."

His dad didn't want to overreact so he kept his cool. But his mother walked into the room and heard Jackson say that he had another child on the way and got excited. She loved grandkids and always wanted a lot.

"Awwww…I'm so excited! You and Tianna need to get married. I don't want my grandbabies coming into this world as bastard children."

"Mama…

"When is she due? I hope it's a granddaughter. I'm going to buy her all these cute little dresses like I used to for Tasha."

Sharon went on and on, she wasn't listening or trying to hear. She was so excited. No matter how many times Jackson tried to stop his mother from talking, she wouldn't. She was too excited about her second grandchild.

The doorbell rang and finally got Sharon's attention. She left the man cave to answer the door and found Tianna and Tyler. She hugged Tianna tight because she'd heard about the baby, although she didn't mention it. She picked up Tyler and kissed him on his cheek. She wanted Tianna to tell her the good news. Tasha and Darren pulled up within minutes of Tianna. She hugged and greeted them as well. They all went inside the home.

"Everyone is right on time. The food is ready to be served. Tianna and Tasha, could you ladies help me in the kitchen? Darren, the guys are in the man cave, but could you tell them that the food will be served in about five minutes?"

Sharon hugged Tianna again and Tianna was baffled as to why she kept hugging her.

"Mama, why you keep hugging her?" Tasha felt left out since she was *her* daughter, but Tianna was getting all the love and hugs.

Sharon explained how Tianna was like a daughter to her and she was proud to have a grandchild.

Darren walked to the man cave and gave Jackson and Adonis the message about dinner. He noticed that Jackson looked disheveled and worried. His dad looked the same. Darren didn't know whether to talk about the game on TV or not. He sat on the sofa across from Jackson.

"So, what up fellas?"

"What's up, D?"

"How you doing, Darren?" Adonis asked.

When each of them was exchanging pleasantries, Tyler ran into the man cave to tell them that his grandma said to wash up because the food was ready.

Jackson grabbed his son to spin him around. He was so happy to see him. He began tickling him.

"Father, father…" were all the words Tyler could get out. He was wrapped up in laughter.

Jackson was elated to hear his son call him father. He usually called him by his first name, so to hear "father" made him realize that he was a father, soon to be father to another child. The thought brought sadness to him, not because of the child but the mother. He couldn't bond with the unborn child because he didn't love Roxanne. In fact, he couldn't stand to be near her. Especially after she spiked his drink.

"Tylerrrr, how you doing?" Adonis asked with emphasis as he rubbed his hand playfully across his head.

Darren gave Tyler a little hand technique known as "dap." Tyler enjoyed all the attention he was getting from his family in Texas. He enjoyed Texas more than Boston and asked his mother if they could move there to be near his family. Tianna pondered the thought, but she couldn't because of school. She knew that he wanted to be around his grandparents and knew he needed to be there as well.

"Dinner is ready!" Tasha yelled from the dining room.
Sharon never lost her touch when it came to cooking. The entire house smelled of pot roast, collard greens, broccoli, garlic baked potatoes, macaroni and cheese, and cornbread.

Jackson and Tyler sat on opposite sides of Tianna. Darren and Tasha sat next to each other while Adonis and Sharon occupied the ends of the table. The cherry wood dining set could be adjusted to the number of patrons' seating.

Tianna hasn't really communicated with Jackson since the Roxanne incident. He called many nights, but she was always busy or short lipped. His time was spent talking to his son instead of Tianna. He invited her to dinner because he wanted to tell them about Roxanne and get it out in the open. He didn't want any secrets between him and his family. Jackson was going to man up.

Food was dropping out of Tyler's mouth it was so good. He couldn't finish chewing because he wanted to ask an important question. So, he asked,

"Grandma and Grandpa, can I stay here with you *forever*?"

Sharon wiped her mouth and quickly answered. She told him that of course he could live with them forever if his mother and father approved.

"Father and Mommy, can I? Please?" he pleaded.

Tasha thought it was a good idea because it would give Tianna time for her studies and to maybe add another course to finish school faster.

Jackson wanted to be near his son and wanted him to live with him, but if he wanted to stay with his parents, he wouldn't object because at least he would be able to see his son daily and even tuck him into bed. And they could continue to build their father and son relationship. But if Jackson had his wish, he would marry Tianna and buy a bigger home for them.

Tianna thought about what everyone was saying. Adding another course would shorten her expected graduation date by a full year. She was still unclear about her and Jackson's relationship because of Roxanne, but she loved him. She could get past Roxanne if she knew for sure that Jackson didn't cheat on her. She was willing to fight for the relationship, but cheating was unacceptable.

Adonis assured Tianna that Tyler would be in good hands. He was retired and could take him fishing, enroll him into sports, and teach him all about being a gentleman.

What they were offering Tianna was difficult to turn down. She loved her son and wanted the best for him. She wouldn't have to worry about anyone harming or kidnapping him in Texas. She could worry less about his welfare if he was in San Antonio. The only thing holding her decision back was that she would miss him like crazy.

"Are you all sure you will take care of him?"

"Of course," Sharon assured Tianna.

"Mommy, please? Can I?"

Tianna looked at Tyler and then at Jackson. She asked Jackson, "Is it okay with you?"

"He's our son. I want to be with him and *you*," Jackson said as he touched Tianna's hand.

Tianna couldn't look into Jackson's eyes. She loved him too much and he would know. The fact that she loved him would never be the reason to be disloyal though or take her love for granted. She wanted to make it clear. She removed her hand from his and said,

"Why don't we let him stay until the end of summer, and then we could see how it goes?"

Tyler was so excited that he hopped out his seat and started running around the dinner table.

"I'm staying here *forever*," he kept chanting.

"I didn't say forever," Tianna reiterated. Tyler didn't understand. The only thing he cared about was that he was staying.

Everyone laughed.

"That boy got too much energy for me," Tasha said.

Tyler was done eating so he asked if he could go in the man cave to play. Jackson approved because he had to tell the family about his unborn child, and he didn't want him to hear grown folks' conversation.

"Wash your hands and then you can go play," Tianna said.

Tyler ran to the downstairs bathroom to wash his hands. He stood on a small stoop that Sharon bought for him the day he spent time with them. When he was done drying his hand. He ran into the man cave.

When Tyler was out of sight, Jackson moved closer to Tianna. She was uncomfortable with him so near because she still wasn't accustomed to the family knowing about them. She wanted to still be seen as the sweet and innocent Tianna from high school. She cleared her throat like something was in her airway.

Tianna's phone beeped with a text message. There was an attachment sent from Michelle.

A text message that read:

Michelle: Girllllll, WTH?

Tianna tried opening the attachment, but it wouldn't open.

"Tianna, can you turn your phone off for a minute? I have something important to say," Jackson said.

Sharon sat there about to jump out of her seat. She was ready to hear how Tianna was pregnant with her second grandchild.

Tianna didn't turn off her phone, but she put it on vibrate and set it on the table.

"Oh, Lord, this should be good," Tasha said as Darren gave her a look that said, *It's not the right time.*

"Jackson, hurry up before I spill the beans." Sharon clapped with excitement. She was the only happy one at the table. Even Adonis had a reserved look on his face.

"Tianna, I have a child on the way," Jackson said as Tianna's phone vibrated. She picked up the phone and the attachment that she tried to open finally downloaded. She saw a Facebook post of a naked Jackson and Roxanne holding her tummy that read, "Jackson Jr." She covered her mouth and began to cry.

"Tianna, what's wrong?" Tasha asked as she picked up the phone to see what Tianna saw.

She showed the phone to Jackson and he put his head down and said, "This is what I've been trying to tell you and everyone."

"What do you mean, you 'have a child on the way'? Isn't Tianna pregnant?" Sharon asked.

"No, Mama, it's not Tianna. It's a woman named Roxanne."

"Yeah, Mama, she's a white girl." Tasha said.

"What?" Adonis, Darren, and Sharon said in unison.

Filled with disappointment, Jackson told them all about his relationship with Roxanne. He told them about her spiking his drink and taking the photos. He claimed that he never slept with her after reuniting with Tianna and Tyler. He didn't love Roxanne and he'd gotten caught up.

"Baby, I never cheated on you. I love you." He pleaded with Tianna.

Tianna didn't want to hear it. She told him not to touch her and that the engagement was off. He'd better get to know Roxanne and his unborn child.

She got up from the table and called for Tyler. Sharon stopped her and took her into a separate room to talk to her like a mother. She knew her son was wrong but that he loved Tianna. She advised her to take some time to hear him out before she made a rash decision that could be a long-term mistake.

"I'm sorry, Mrs. Norwood, I can't and would never accept a man that cheated on me and created another child."

Jackson walked into the room with Tianna and his mother. He wasn't letting her go until he explained to her that the child was created *before* they reunited.

"No, Jackson. Let me go. Don't touch me."

"Mommy, what's wrong? Father, what are you doing to my Mommy?" Tyler cried out as he heard his mother crying from the man cave. He came to check on her.

"Son, go into the room and continue playing. Mommy and I are just talking."

"Nooo, what's wrong, Mommy?"

"Mommy is okay, now do what your father asked you." Tianna assured her son.

Tasha walked into the room to take Tyler out, even though she wanted to intervene and curse her brother out. She felt Tianna's pain. What Jackson did was not forgivable.

Tyler left the room with Tasha, and she, Darren, and Adonis stayed with him inside the man cave until everyone calmed down. Everyone was calm except for Tianna.

She couldn't look at Jackson, her entire world had been turned upside down. She was going to be his wife and bear *all* his children. They were going to be a family. Now, they had to welcome another child by another woman into their family. She wasn't ready for it, nor would she ever be. Roxanne had stripped her of her "happily ever after."

She went to the man cave to get her son so they could leave.

Everyone stared at her, but she said nothing. She was so upset and stomped like a child. Her three-inch heels could be heard loud and thunderous on the hardwood floors.

"Tianna, you are not walking out of my life again or taking my son away from me!" Jackson cried while trailing her every step.

"You're right, I'm not walking out of your life. You pushed me out," she said as she opened the front door to leave.

"Tianna, I love you and my son," Jackson pleaded.

Adonis came next to his son to place his arms around him and said, "Son, let her go."

Jackson rested his head on his dad's shoulder and cried like a man as he watched the woman he loved drive away.

Chapter Fifteen

Bernadette helped Tianna pack her things. She hated to see her daughter leave in such a state of mind. She knew that Tyler would be staying with the Norwoods for the summer so she could pick him up whenever she was off. She told Tianna that she would check on him regularly.

Tianna wasn't really worried about Tyler's well-being because she knew he was in good hands. She trusted the Norwoods with her life.

Tianna picked up her phone. There were ten missed calls. Nine of them were from Jackson and the other was from Jamal wanting to get with her before she left town.

She returned Jamal's call and made plans for him to come over and get take-out food and watch a movie.

"Mama, Jamal is coming over to spend time with Tyler and me before I leave. We are going to watch movies."

"I've always liked Jamal. He's the one that really loves you. You won't hear of Jamal getting white girls pregnant. He knows how to keep his penis in his pants, unlike Jackson.

"Mama, I don't want to bash my son's father. Just let it go."

"I ain't letting nothing go. I told you Jackson wasn't no damn good."

Grandma Debby overheard Tianna and Bernadette talking. She entered the room to give her opinion about the entire ordeal of Jackson cheating. She didn't have any ill feelings against him. She knew that he truly loved her granddaughter. She'd witnessed it many times when Tianna was in high school.

She still had faith in Jackson that he was the one for her grandbaby. She prayed that Tianna and Jackson could work out their differences for Tyler's sake.

Jackson was successful and could take care of them. She knew that Jamal loved Tianna, too, but Tianna was in love with Jackson. Her heart belonged to him. She wanted her to be happy.

She hated seeing her granddaughter mope around the house when she should be enjoying her spring break vacation.

She wished she could take away her pain but knew how complicated and difficult relationships were. She'd divorced Bernadette's father for cheating but then forgave him and they remarried. They were together for over twenty years until his death. She had first-hand experience on how relationships could be reconciled after infidelity. It was not easy, but it wasn't impossible.

Debby waited until Bernadette left the room so she and Tianna could have a woman to woman talk about men. She revealed a lot about her life with her husband. Tianna was shocked to hear the things about her grandpa. She'd never known that he cheated or that they remarried.

Her grandma advised her to think things through before she gave up on Jackson. She knew genuine love when she saw it. Debby told her that technically Jackson didn't cheat since they were not together during the time he was messing with the white girl.

Tianna knew he didn't cheat but it was the fact that Roxanne was *pregnant* and she wanted to have all of Jackson's children. It would be difficult to accept an outside child.

"That's not that child's fault. Children don't ask to be in this world. You will learn to love that child as your own."

Tianna knew she was being selfish, but she didn't care. She loved Jackson but Roxanne and her unborn child was too much for her to accept right now.

The doorbell rang and Bernadette answered. Jamal stood at the front door. She stepped aside and invited him in. She asked about his ankle and how he was doing. They talked for about five minutes before Tyler saw him.

"Hi, Daddy. I miss you!" Tyler screamed as he ran to jump on him.

"I miss you more, he said as he spun Tyler gingerly around. He still hadn't fully recovered from his ankle sprain.

"Tianna is in her room packing. You can wait down here for her or you can go upstairs if you can make it."

"Thanks, Ms. Thompson. I can make it upstairs."

"That's Ms. Bernadette, I'm not an old woman."

"Sorry Ms. Bernadette."

Bernadette told everyone to call her by her first name and not last. She always thought of herself as young since she had Tianna at seventeen. She didn't look old and was still beautiful. She looked more like Tianna's older sister than her mother.

"Daddy, I can help you."

"That won't be necessary. Hey, Jamal," Tianna said as she came down the stairs.

Grandma Debby was behind her and greeted Jamal. She didn't have anything against Jamal but she favored Jackson a little bit more.

"Did you bring the movies or do we need to go rent them?" Tianna asked.

"We can go rent some or we could go out to a movie."

"I want to go to the movies," Tyler said as he jumped up and down. He was so full of energy.

"Your father will be here in a minute to pick you up." Tianna told her son.

"He could go with us and then we can drop him off after the movie. I want to spend some time with my son," Jamal said with a pleading look.

Tianna thought about it, and with her mother and grandmother's approval, she decided to call Jackson to let him know of the change of plans.

Tianna, Tyler, and Jamal bid farewell to Bernadette and Debby and were on their way to the movies when Jackson pulled up in front of the house. Jackson was pissed when he saw Tianna and Tyler enter Jamal's black Ford F250. He parked his car behind Jamal's and blocked them in.

Tianna huffed and grabbed for the door handle when Jamal stopped her and said that he would handle it. Jamal opened his door when Tianna stopped him and said that she would talk to him and let him know of the plans.

She got out and met Jackson half-way between his car and Jamal's truck and out of Tyler and Jamal's hearing range.

"I tried to call you to let you know that we had a change of plans. I will drop Tyler off later tonight after the movies," she said.

"Jamal, good old boy always to the rescue. When is he going to get it?"

"Get what?"

"That you never wanted him and that it has always been about *me*."

"Don't flatter yourself, we are no longer teenagers."

Jackson got square into Tianna's face to let her know that he may have messed up but he was never going to give up on her and that they would get married because it was intended for them to be together. And the only reason he wasn't starting anything with Jamal was because his son was in the truck. He wanted to be a good role model for him, and it was lucky for Jamal because he would break his other ankle to keep him away from his family.

He pulled Tianna near, grabbing her butt and kissed her lips. She reluctantly obliged, and although she was angry, she felt her guard shiver like a feather. She was so weak behind him.

When Jamal saw that Tianna didn't resist, he immediately got out the truck. He wasn't going to sit there and watch Jackson Norwood steal his woman again.

Tyler didn't notice any of it, he was too busy in the back seat playing his Nintendo 3DS.

"What's up, Leftovers. I mean, Jamal?" Jackson said as he turned his attention away from Tianna but still held his arm around her waist.

"That's what I came to find out. How's your baby mama?" Jamal hissed.

"She's standing right here and as far as I can see. She's fine," Jackson said as he looked at Tianna's ass and gave it a little pat.

"Jackson, stop," Tianna finally said.

"Naw, I was talking about your *white* baby mama." Jamal smirked. Jackson didn't know that Tianna told him about Roxanne.

"All right, that's enough." Tianna intervened.

She told Jackson that she would drop Tyler off after the movie.

He didn't really want to adhere to her request but did so to keep the peace. She asked Jamal to go back to the truck so she could talk to Jackson about Tyler staying with him for the summer. He reluctantly walked back to the truck and sat inside waiting for Tianna.

Jackson talked about the arrangements and continued to confess his love for her, letting her know that he would do everything in his power to win her back and right his wrong. She didn't want to hear it. In her book, it was officially over. But in her heart, it would never be over and it would always be unfinished business between them.

Tianna walked to Jamal's truck and Jackson walked behind her to talk to his son and tell him that he would see him later. He gave Jamal a look of disgust and tried to give Tianna one last kiss, but she stopped him. This made Jamal elated as Tianna got in, and he put the truck in drive as Jackson stood there hotter than fish grease. He didn't even get to see his son. He was so upset but tried to be cool. He couldn't watch another man drive off with his family.

Grandma Debby and Bernadette stared out the window at the entire exchange. Debby went outside to talk to Jackson before he drove off. She gave him hope that he, Tyler, and Tianna would still be a family.

Tianna wished they had stayed home and rented a movie instead of going out. Jamal was so popular that he spent the entire night signing autographs for his fans. They took pictures with him and some with his son. Tianna was in a few but didn't care for the limelight. She wanted a simple life where she could go anywhere she pleased without the cameras.

"Jamal, is she your girlfriend? One of his female fans asked. Jamal smiled and said,

"Yes, she is."

Tianna didn't say anything but smiled. She didn't want to embarrass him, but she was going to tell him when they got some privacy. Tyler loved taking pictures and interacting with the fans. He was a natural and enjoyed it, but maybe he was a little too young to understand what was going on.

Tianna and Jamal went to get Tyler's luggage and dropped him off at the Norwood's house. She didn't want to take him directly to Jackson because she didn't want him to start with Jamal and she was worn out from the movie. She avoided all of Jackson's drama. She was leaving in the morning and wanted to get a good night's sleep.

When Jamal pulled up at Tianna's mother's house to walk her inside, Jackson was parked in front listening to his playlist. His head rested on the headrest like he was tired and worried.

Tianna got out of the truck to bid Jamal farewell, but he insisted on walking her inside to get her away from Jackson. She declined and told him that she would be fine and that she really wanted to get some sleep before the flight in the morning. He asked to drive her to the airport, but her mother was driving her. He left reluctantly, but not without giving her a goodnight hug and kiss.

"You know you don't love him, so why you frontin'?" Jackson said as he got out of his car.

"Jackson, not tonight. I'm tired."

"Where's my son? I thought you were bringing him by my house?"

"I didn't want to deal with you, so I dropped him at your parents'," Tianna said as she kept walking toward the front door.

"I need to talk to you. Just give me five minutes," Jackson pleaded.

Tianna unlocked the door and he followed her inside. She walked to her room and turned on the TV. She began taking off her coat and shoes. Jackson did the same.

"What are you doing?" She asked. She was only giving him five minutes, but he sat on the bed next to her undressing as if he was staying the night.

"Go ahead and take your shower. I'll wait until you get out and that's when my five minutes begins."

"Jackson, I'm not about to play with you," Tianna said as she walked into her bathroom to fully undress. She didn't want Jackson to see the scars that were left on her body from Mark.

Each day she looked in the mirror it reminded her of that brutal night. She took off her make-up and brushed her teeth before she entered the shower. She heard Jackson messing with her CD player. She recognized his playlist. She saw no light from the TV glaring under the bathroom door.

What is he up to? She thought to herself when she saw the doorknob turn and the door opened. There Jackson stood, naked as a jaybird. The song, "Lose Control" by Silk was playing in the background on his iPhone. Tianna grabbed the shower curtain to cover herself, but he kept walking toward her.

"Jackson what are you doing?"

"I'm about to take a shower with *my* fiancée."

He took the shower curtain from around her and saw her body. He wanted to break inside the jailhouse to kill Mark. He saw the look of embarrassment on Tianna's face, but instead of making her feel self-conscience about her scars, he walked inside the shower and pressed his body close to hers and took her into his arms. She laid on his shoulder and he held her tight.

He broke the embrace and looked into her dark beaded eyes and asked,

"Is my *five minutes* up?"

Tianna shook her head side to side meaning "no," but she whispered a soft gentle "yes" that he couldn't hear.

He lifted her chin to meet his eyes as he licked the side of her cheek like a dog.

"Jackson, you're so crazy." She laughed.

"But you love it, right?"

"I didn't say all thatttt." She giggled like a schoolgirl.

He licked the other cheek and spread her legs with his knee. He kissed her forehead and then traced her dark brown eyelashes and eyes with his tongue followed by gentle kisses. She knew what was about to happen but couldn't stop it. She wanted him just as much as he wanted her. She loved him and he loved her. He was going to give her something to remember before she left for Boston in the morning and he did just that. He loved her throughout the night until the morning. Their love making was so intense that they only got two hours of sleep before her departure.

Jackson took Tianna to the airport. He didn't want to let her go as his heart cried for her. But she had unfinished business at Harvard University and had to leave. Her phone beeped with a missed call from Jamal followed by a message. Jamal had stayed around the corner after dropping Tianna off the previous night. He left after Jackson's car didn't move for over an hour. He knew that Jackson stayed the night with her.

She ignored his message and kept her attention on the man she loved.

"You know I'm not on any birth control pills," Tianna whispered to him since they were talking about their night together on the way to the airport.

"Yeah, I know. And neither am I," Jackson said playfully as he pulled out his Ray-Ban glasses and put them on to block the sun. He was so damn gorgeous when he wore his glasses. Tianna didn't know if he wore them because of the sun rays or for the sex appeal. Whichever it was, he wore them well.

She couldn't resist his witty charm and told him that it was going to be the end of them having *unprotected* sex. He disagreed and pulled her close by grabbing her rear end and told her that she was having all his children and Tyler was just the first.

He loved her butt and couldn't help but grab it every time she was near. She loved his outspoken demeanor. He knew what he wanted, and he was coming to get it.

Tyler was just the first, she thought to herself before she entered the terminal to get to her plane.

He told her that he would see her soon and that he would be in Boston within a week. She didn't want him to come only because she knew that he was irresistible and she couldn't focus on her school work. She wanted to finish school and move back to Texas.

He wanted marriage and a family sooner rather than later. And his *sooner* was different from hers. He didn't want to waste any time. They embraced and kissed for the last time.

"Take care of my baby. I will call you when I get home," she said as she waved him goodbye. He waited until her airplane took off before he left.

He watched her plane in the air until it was out of sight.

His phone beeped with a text message from Roxanne,

Roxanne: Hey baby daddy. I will c u tonight when you cum over. R. She included a kissy face heart emoji at the end.

Chapter Sixteen

Tianna arrived in Boston approximately five hours later.

Michelle and Malcolm picked her up from the airport. They already missed Tyler and couldn't believe Tianna let him stay for the summer. She didn't want him to stay but she could get a lot of things done, like staying in the library or joining a late-night study group to help her get through the more intense classes. She didn't have to rush to the day care center to get him. She only had to look after herself and wouldn't have to worry about Mark kidnapping her child. Even though he was being sentenced to twenty years in prison without parole eligibility until he served fifteen years.

The judge didn't go lenient on him this time despite his parents' pleas or clout within the judicial system.

Tianna had seen Markette, Mark's twin sister, the year before in Walmart and she was pregnant. They didn't say anything to each other and went their separate ways.

Markette was just like Mark and his father. Tianna felt sorry for the man that married her because he married into a corrupt and deranged family.

She was deep in her thoughts when Michelle asked her about the pictures of Roxanne and Jackson. Michelle saw the pictures on Facebook from a mutual friend of Roxanne's.

She wanted to forget all about Roxanne, especially about the pictures she took when she drugged him.

"You know she put GHB in Jackson's drink when she took those pictures?"

"Girl, no she didn't. He was messing with that woman."

"How do you know?"

"Because he's a dog. And you should be engaged to Jamal. Instead, you chose the dog with the fleas."

"Michelle, you don't know so stop instigating stuff," X intervened.

"I know that Jackson don't deserve her."

Maybe Michelle was right about Jackson. She knew that she had to decide soon about Jackson and Jamal. She didn't want to lead either astray. She loved both but Jamal has been the most trustworthy. The one that always had her back and been by her side through thick and thin. She had so much love and respect for him. But Jackson was her fiancé and they had a child together. She loved him. She craved him. He was the one for her.

But how could she know for sure that he was the one? When she never gave Jamal a chance? Speaking of Jamal, she needed to return his call as soon as possible.

Jackson pulled into the parking lot of his job. He noticed Roxanne standing outside her car waiting for him. He turned off his music and killed the car engine. He looked at her and she had tears in her eyes. He couldn't stand to see a woman cry. Besides, she was the mother of his child, whether he liked it or not. She deserved a little bit of respect.

"What's going on?" he asked with concern.

"I've been spotting blood all morning, Jackson. I don't want to lose the baby," she said as she threw herself into his arms. It caught him off guard, but he held her trying to comfort her.

"Will you go to the doctor with me?"

"I have to find someone to replace me. You know I can't just take off whenever I want to without someone at the pharmacy."

"I know. That's why I called Stephen to see if he could work for you. He said that he would, but you owe him one."

Jackson gasped because he didn't want Roxanne making any kind of decisions for him. She wasn't his girl. But he wanted to make sure that his unborn child was okay.

He reluctantly obliged and opened the car door for her and they were on their way to the doctor to check on his child.

When they got to Dr. Peters's office, there was a waiting room full of pregnant women. A few had their husbands with them but most of them were alone. He was glad that he decided to go with Roxanne because he didn't want to abandon his responsibilities.

As soon as they walked in to take a seat, a Black woman whispered to her friend,

"Humpf, look at him with that Becky."

Jackson wanted to explain to them that "Becky" wasn't his woman, and they were not together, but didn't feel that he could explain how he got Roxanne pregnant if they weren't.

Roxanne signed the sign-in sheet and waited until the medical assistant called her name.

While they were checking her vitals, one of the Black girls walked up to Jackson and asked him what white girls had that Black women didn't?

He was taken aback by her question and decided to tell them how he got caught up and that white women were not his choice. He was engaged to a Black woman and had a child with her.

"What are you doing here with Becky then?"

"I'm a man that owns up to my mistakes and responsibilities. Roxanne didn't create the child alone and I want to do the right thing. By the way, her name is Roxanne not Becky."

"You are a good brother then, and they are hard to find. I'm glad you're owning up but what does your fiancée think about you being here with her?"

"She is in Boston studying to get her Harvard law degree, so she doesn't know that I'm here."

Jackson conversed with the two women until Roxanne called him back to the room because the doctor wanted to do a sonogram.

He helped Roxanne disrobe and change into the gown provided by the doctor's office. She lay on the table while a gel was spread across her tummy. Dr. Peters stated that the dark spot was the baby. They heard a strong heartbeat and Roxanne breathed a sigh of relief. The baby wasn't developed since she was only three months pregnant.

When Roxanne took off her clothes, Jackson noticed that he didn't see the birthmark on her left breast. He ignored it and kept looking at the monitor to make sure his child wasn't in danger. The doctor assured them that everything looked fine, and that some women have spotting, but if it didn't continue then there was nothing to be concerned about. He advised her to relax and stop stressing. She got dressed and took his advice.

When Jackson and Roxanne left the office, one of the Black women said bye and it was a pleasure talking with him. This got Roxanne upset and jealous, but she tried not to show it. She was carrying *his* child and they were forever going to be connected. Roxanne placed her arm in Jackson's arm, gave the women a sly sinister smile, and waved goodbye.

Jackson opened the door and Roxanne walked in front of him. They got into his car and drove off. Before he took her back to her car at work, they stopped to get something to eat at the Olive Garden. They ate and then left. He embraced her out of respect for his child and watched her drive away. He went inside his workplace to check and make sure Stephen was fine with covering for him and to relieve him if need be. Stephen did have some personal business to attend to, so he thanked Jackson for coming in.

"All right man, I got you."

"Hey man, before I forget to tell you. Roxanne is going around telling everyone that she's pregnant with your child."

"Yeah man, I got caught up."

"Do you know if it's yours? I heard that she's out there."

"She says it is, but I will get a DNA test done once the child is born," Jackson assured him.

"Straight up, man. These women are wilding out here putting these brothers on child support and they're not the daddy."

"Thanks for your concern and filling in for me."

"Peace, brother," Stephen said before he left for the day.

Tianna was asleep when her cell phone and landline started ringing. She forgot that Michelle and X were attending his rally later that day and there was no one home but her. She was tired from her and Jackson's love making session in the shower and didn't get much sleep. Include the jet lag into the equation and she was dead tired. She answered the phone in a groggy voice when Jamal blurted out,

"I guess your boy didn't waste no time getting back to his old ways."

"Jamal, what are you talking about? And who's my boy?"

"Jackson, I just saw him with his white baby mama out at the Olive Garden eating."

"Jamal, stop playing with me."

"I ain't playing. Check your messages on your phone."

She saw pictures of Jackson and Roxanne sitting at the table eating and smiling. Jamal took pictures of their embrace and him opening the door for her.

Tianna couldn't believe it. She began to cry. How could she let her guard down and Jackson continue to screw her over?

"I told you that he doesn't love you, beautiful. And you deserve better. I'm coming to town tomorrow and will need to stay in the guestroom."

Tianna stopped crying when she heard Jamal was coming to town. She was going to pay Jackson back and couldn't wait until Jamal arrived.

She dried her tears and said,

"I can't wait to see you."

"Have a good night, beautiful."

"You too, Jamal," Tianna cooed into the phone.

As soon as they hung up, Tianna took her phone, looked at the pictures, and yelled into it.

"Damn, you, Jackson Jeffrey Norwood! Damn you," she repeated as she cried herself back to sleep.

"I hope you're finally going to leave his no-good ass alone," Michelle said as she looked at the pictures of Roxanne and Jackson.

"I'm done this time. He's been calling me all night and day and I haven't answered. I don't know if it's Tyler though? I will call him to make sure."

Tianna's cell phone rang and it displayed Jackson calling. Michelle offered to answer it and curse him out, but Tianna talked her out of it. She'd answer and give him a piece of her mind.

"Hello?"

"Mommy, where have you been? I've been calling you all day," Tyler said.

"Hey baby, Mommy has been sleeping. I had a long flight and I was just getting some rest. How are you?"

Before Tyler could answer, Jackson took the phone from him and asked him to go play in his room because he wanted to talk to his mother.

"Father, are you mad at Mommy?"

"No, son, I love Mommy. I could never be mad at her."

"Promise me?"

"I promise," Jackson assured his son before he ran off to his room.

Tianna heard the conversation between Tyler and Jackson and it melted her heart. She loved him but she wasn't going to stand for him cheating on her with his other baby mama.

She wanted to hang up in his face but also wanted to hear him out.

"Hey baby, are you okay? We've been calling you all night and day."

"Yes, I'm fine," she hissed with attitude.

"Why didn't you answer the phone? We left several messages."

"Don't try to act so innocent, Jackson. I saw the pictures."

"What pictures?"

Michelle couldn't believe Tianna's reaction and wanted to press end on the phone herself.

Jackson could hear Michelle in the background: "Good for nothing. Why doesn't he stay with that white bitch and leave you alone?" He didn't know what was going on or what Michelle was talking about.

"Tianna, what is going on? Baby?" he asked before Michelle took the phone from Tianna and yelled, "Dirty bastard!" and hung up.

Jackson called back several times but got no response. He texted her:

Jackson: Baby, what's wrong? I didn't do anything. Please pick up the phone.

Jackson: Tianna, what did I do?

Jackson: Please baby, please, pick up the phone. We need to talk.

Jackson: Tianna, please talk to me.

Jackson: I love u.

He went on and on and he could see that she read each message he sent because of the send receipts.

She responded with the photos that Jamal sent. He waited for the pictures to download and saw himself with Roxanne the day he took her to her doctor's appointment.

Jackson: Tianna, that's not what u think!!!!

Tianna: It's over Jackson, don't call me unless it is about our son.

Jackson: Baby, don't do this to me, again! I love u!!!!

Jackson: I'm crazy abt u. Please talk to me!! Let me explain.

Tianna: Goodnight and goodbye, Jackson.

Chapter Seventeen

It had been months since Tianna had spoken to Jackson. She conversed with her son when he was at the Norwoods or her mother's home. She knew that Jackson took Tyler to Disneyland for his birthday. She talked to him a day before his birthday and on the day before the trip. When he was with Jackson, she rarely answered her phone. She missed and loved Jackson, but it was time for her to let him go. She had been seriously dating Jamal since her and Jackson's breakup. He fully recovered from his ankle and was back with the Spurs. He flew down on his off days to see her. Jamal visited his son when he was in Texas and gave Tasha and Darren tickets to bring Tyler to his games.

The Norwoods were cool with him visiting and knew that Jamal took care of Tyler for over four years and didn't want to interfere with their bonding. They loved Jamal like a son and trusted him.

"I see you and Jamal getting *real* serious, huh?" Michelle asked as she came out of her room to talk to Tianna.

Tianna was on her way to school early because she needed to meet with Professor Green about her test score.

"Yes, we are. I think he's about ready to pop the question." Tianna smiled.

"Well, it's about time and you better say 'yes'!"

"We will see," Tianna said as she grabbed her backpack and slug it across her back.

It was finals at school and Tianna was pressed for time on her studies. Her love for Jamal was growing stronger and stronger. He called her every day or sent a text message to make sure she knew how much he loved her. She returned the same sentiments.

She was flying to Texas in the morning since her last exam was that day. She would be at his game with Tyler on Saturday night when he played her least favorite team, the Lakers.
She'd never liked the Lakers but had more disdain for them ever since Kobe raped that young woman in Denver, Colorado. And got away with it. She hated how the sports world just swept that incident under the rug because he was the greatest superstar in basketball. She loathed him, and

his wife Vanessa for taking him back. She thought Vanessa was spineless and only wanted Kobe for a meal ticket.

She was glad that Jamal didn't idolize Kobe and wanted to be nothing like him. Jamal was his own man and didn't look up to any superstar. He said that they were men like him and put their pants on one leg at a time like he did. There was no need to jock another dude.

"Michelle, I'll see you later tonight. I may need you to take me to the airport tomorrow if you don't have plans."

"What time?"

"My flight departs at nine in the morning."

"Oh yeah, I can take you. I'm not doing anything for the break. In fact, I may take a few summer courses."

"Girl, more power to you. I wish I could handle your course load," Tianna said before she left for school.

She got in her car and turned the radio on 98.5 Old School Jams. Aaliyah's "Let me know" was playing. She couldn't help but think of high school and Jackson giving her and Jamal a ride the day he played her song. She looked into her rearview mirror, reflecting on the way Jackson had looked at her in the backseat of his car. She smiled at the memories.

Her phone rang through the hands-free set in her BMW.

"Hey, T, What are you doing?"

"Hey Tasha, I'm on my way to class. Where have you been?"

"I've been busy and struggling through some womanhood woes."

"What you mean, womanhood woes?"

"Darren and I are ready to have a family and we've tried for months and I haven't got pregnant."

"Awwww, Tash, I'm sorry. But it will happen when the time is right."

"I know, but I'm ready now. I see all these kids running around, and talking with them daily makes me even more anxious to have some of my own."

Tasha wanted to be a child psychologist after her accident but didn't know how much of a toll it would take on her mentally and physically.

She encountered all types of children with different backgrounds and heard many stories of abuse. She couldn't help them all but wanted to.

"I will call or see you when I get here this weekend," Tianna said.

"Oh, I didn't know you were coming to town. Call me if you need me to pick you up from the airport. What time are you landing?"

"I should be there by the afternoon."

"Oh, before I forget, did you know my brother opened his own pharmacy? He's working for himself."

"Wow, that's really nice. I'm happy to hear that and proud of him."

"Can I ask you a question, and can you be honest with me?"

"Sure, anything."

"Do you still love Jackson?"

"Tasha, what kind of question is that? He's my son's father."

"Yeah, I know. But do you love him outside of being Tyler's father?"

Tianna drove through a tunnel when she was about to answer, lost her connection, and the phone died. She was at school and decided to call Tasha later. She didn't want anything to distract her from doing well on her final exams. She parked her car in student parking and walked to Professor Green's office before her first exam. He wasn't expecting her but was still able to converse with her about her test score. Tianna was one of his favorite students because she challenged him in debates. She wasn't afraid to question him. She stood her ground and he liked that. She wanted to see why her answers were given half-credit instead of full. He tried to explain the best he could, but she eventually won. She walked out of his office with full-credit and an A on his exam.

She walked through the courtyard and saw X.

"Hey Tianna, you good?"

"Oh yes, I'm good. I just left Professor Green's office to challenge my grade and got my A on the exam and in the class."

"That's my girl," X said as he gave her a hug.

"I'll see you later tonight."

"All right, catch you later," X said as he pulled out the plastic hair pick from his pocket and stuck it into his Afro.

Tianna shook her head, admiring that X didn't give a damn. He was pro-Black and didn't care what people thought of him.

There were over one hundred people at the grand opening of Jackson & Tyler Pharmacy.

Jackson named his pharmacy in dedication to his first-born son. The Norwoods, Tyler, Tasha, Darren, people from church, and the neighborhood came out to celebrate the opening of their new local pharmacy.

Jackson held Tyler's hand as they both cut the red ribbon and the crowd cheered. Jackson picked his son up and put him around his neck. Tyler was over six feet tall sitting on top of his father's neck. He clapped and cheered along with the crowd.

Everyone walked inside the pharmacy to take an up close and personal look. There was plenty of space for medicines and counseling cubicles for his patients. Jackson hired two pharmacy assistants from the company he used to work for. He was giving them better benefits and pay, but most importantly, an opportunity to serve the Black community, and help the elderly afford their medicines. He hired another pharmacist on a part-time basis to relieve him when he wanted to take a vacation. But he was the primary pharmacist in charge and on duty most days.

"Son, I'm so proud of you," his father said.

"Me too," Sharon exclaimed.

Mrs. Brown from the church came up to Jackson and said how much he'd grown into a handsome, intelligent young man and that she'd seen it in him since he was a little boy.

"Thank you, Mrs. Brown. And thank you for coming out today to celebrate."

"It was my pleasure, baby. Now where is Tianna? How come she isn't here?"

"She's at school finishing her law degree."

"Oh, it's a shame she missed your special day."

Jackson didn't tell anyone that he and Tianna were no longer together or the fact that he was having a child with another woman was the reason they broke up. In fact, he didn't want to talk about her. He wanted time to heal and dedicated himself to his son and work. It was helping him cope.

"Hey Jackson, congratulations, man, you did it. You know if you need some software programs, I'm your man," Darren said.

"Oh yeah, I'm going to be needing a few. I will get with you and set up a good price."

"Man, you know I'm family and I won't charge you. You are doing a lot for this community and it's the least that I can do."

"I appreciate it, brother-in-law."

Tasha came from behind Jackson and hugged him tight. She was so proud of her brother and all that he was going through to still accomplish his dream. He took his inheritance and invested well to make money to open his own business. Their grandmother would be proud if she was still living. She always adored Jackson and he was her pride and joy. She named him because she was a huge fan of the Jackson 5.

"Father, are we going to call Mommy? I want to talk to her?"

"Yes, son. We will call her as soon as we are done here."

"Okay. I miss her."

Jackson wanted to say "me too" but instead refrained from showing his true feelings.

He greeted a few more patrons before he decided to close the doors until the pharmacy was officially ready for business.

He and Tyler stopped at Pizza Hut to buy pizza and hot wings after stopping at GameStop to buy a new video game for his Nintendo 3DS.

Greetings everyone, this is Tianna and I'm not here to take your call so please leave a brief message after the beep.

"Hi, Mommy. I miss you," Tyler spoke into Tianna's voicemail. "I love you. Please give me a call when you get home. This is your son, Tyler."

A few hours passed and there was still no call from Tianna until almost nine o'clock at night. Jackson answered the phone and his heart stuttered when he heard her voice.

"Hey, how are you?" she asked Jackson.

"I'm good, but your son isn't. He has been asking about you all day."

"I'm sorry. I've been so busy with school. Today was my last final exam and I'm flying out to Texas tomorrow morning to see him."

"I'm sure he would like that. Do you want me to wake him up so he can talk to you?"

"No, just let him sleep. I will be there by evening and will give you a call to pick him up."

"Sounds good. Have a good night," Jackson said as he pressed end on his phone.

He walked into the kitchen to pour himself a glass of wine and turned the TV on SportsCenter.

He received a text message from Roxanne asking if she could come over, but he didn't respond. In fact, he turned his phone off so that he wouldn't be bothered by her.

He went upstairs to check on his son before he got into the shower. He kissed him on his forehead and placed the comforter over him. Tyler hadn't brushed his teeth or taken a bath, and if Tianna knew it, she would be upset. But Jackson knew that what she didn't know, didn't hurt.

He closed Tyler's bedroom door and walked to his room.

When he got out of the shower, he heard his doorbell ring. He looked out the peephole and it was Roxanne. He sighed and didn't want to open the door. He let her ring the doorbell for another minute or so hoping that she would get in her car and leave.

He rested his head against the door and thought to himself, *how or why did I get involved with her?*

It was one of his biggest mistakes and it had wreaked havoc in his life. If it wasn't for Roxanne, he and Tianna would be together. He would be holding her tight and making love to her as soon as she arrived in town tomorrow. Instead, he was dealing with Roxanne ringing the doorbell late at night.

"I know you are in there, baby daddy. So why don't you open the fuckin door!"

"Go home, Roxanne. I don't have time for you tonight."

"Oh yeah, well you better make time."

Jackson didn't know what to do with her. He didn't want to call the police on his child's mother, but he wanted her to leave him alone.

If he could shake the baby out of her and get away with it, he would, but that wasn't in his DNA.

He opened the door and she pushed herself inside his house.

"What the hell do you want?"

"That's not the way you talk to Tianna, so why are you talking to me that way? Huh?"

"Look, don't you say *nothing* about Tianna. In fact, don't you mention her. What the hell do you want, like I said?"

"I want you, baby daddy," She said as she grabbed his penis.

"Roxanne, get out of here. I told you already that you are to come around only when my child is born or for doctor's visits. Your appointment isn't until next week, so leave."

"I know you heard my brother, tramp," Tasha said as she walked up to the front door of Jackson's home and heard the exchange between him and Roxanne.

She knew that Jackson couldn't beat her down, and neither could she, but that didn't stop her from making threats to get her away from her brother's house.

Roxanne turned around to see Tasha and her face took on a look that said, "try me if you want to."

She didn't want to try Tasha, so she told Jackson to go screw himself and walked out.

Tasha slammed the door behind her and called her a THOT.

She wanted no part of Roxanne even though she was carrying her niece. Jackson and Roxanne found out that they were having a baby girl.

"What are you doing here?"

"I came by to see you. And to tell you that Tianna will be in Texas tomorrow."

"Yeah, I know. I talked to her a few hours ago."

"She wants me to pick her up from the airport and I came to see if you wanted to go with me?"

"Naw, I'm good. I have to work, and besides, I'm not kissing her ass anymore to be with me. I'm getting stronger each day."

"Wow, I'm proud of you, but I still believe there's hope for the two of you. You know you still love her. I can see it in your eyes."

"Love ain't got nothing to do with it. I'm tired of her believing everybody *but* me. I know I messed up, but I haven't messed with Roxanne since Tianna and I got back together."

"I believe you. But those pictures of you and Roxanne don't seem convincing."

Tasha talked to Jackson for about an hour before she left to go home. She talked about the fertility issues between her and Darren, hoping he could give them advice. He suggested they both get tested to see if her eggs could produce or if Darren had a low sperm count. He told her about taking fertility drugs and said it could be expensive, but worth it if she really wanted a child. He could supply her the medicine if she saw the doctor first.

She thanked him and bid him goodnight.

Chapter Eighteen

Roxanne sat waiting for her cousin Markette's plane to arrive from Boston. She couldn't wait to see her little adorable second cousin, Emily. She kept pacing as if she was anxious or nervous, like she was being stalked or watched by a private investigator.

She always had next to no patience.

She went to Starbucks to get a medium caramel Frappuccino.

While sitting at a table she noticed Tianna walking toward Tasha, waving to get her attention.

Roxanne immediately ducked inside of Starbucks to get out of sight.

When Roxanne tried to dodge Tianna and Tasha that's when she saw Markette pass right by. Markette hissed and rolled her eyes when she saw Tianna.

Roxanne didn't want to say anything until they were out of sight, so she let her cousin wander around looking for her.

She saw Markette pull out her cell phone and figured she would be calling her.

Roxanne's phone rang and she answered immediately.

"Hey Roxy, where are you? I'm here."

"I'm in Starbucks getting a Frappuccino."

Markette turned toward Starbucks and saw Roxanne.

"Oh, I see you," she said before she hung up and met Roxanne half way.

Roxanne took Markette's luggage while she held onto Emily's hand. Emily was fussy and cried almost the entire flight. She had an ear infection and hadn't been feeling good for two days.

Markette almost cancelled her trip to Texas but had already purchased her tickets.

"Hi Emily, how are you feeling?" Roxanne asked.

Emily just looked at her with tears in her eyes rubbing her ear.

"Awww, I know you don't feel good, honey."

Markette picked up Emily so that they could move past the crowd standing and waiting for their loved ones to arrive or depart. When they got to the front doors to leave the airport Markette noticed Tianna again.

"Humpf, look what the wind blew in," Markette said.

Tianna heard Markette but didn't recognize her until she saw Roxanne standing right next to her. Roxanne tried to hide her face, but Tianna saw her. She tapped Tasha to ask if that was Roxanne. Tasha removed her sunglasses and said,

"Yeah that's that tramp. She came over to my brother's house last night. I had to send her home."

"I thought she was four months pregnant. She doesn't look pregnant to me." Tianna said.

"I know she doesn't. Last night when I saw her, her belly was bigger."

"What are y'all Black asses looking at?" Markette barked.

"We're trying to find out," Tasha barked back.

Tianna gave Tasha a slight push telling her to go because they were not worth a criminal record. She knew that Markette and Roxanne would be cleared of all charges but they wouldn't be.

"Yeah, you right. They lucky," Tasha said before she stepped off the curb and into the parking lot to locate her Mercedes.

She huffed a few more obscenities looking back at Markette, but she wanted to respect her little girl, who looked sick. So she chilled and changed the subject.

Tianna expressed to Tasha how much she missed Tyler, but she was able to get a lot of things done without him.

"I know that may sound bad as a mother, but I'm so glad that your family kept him."

"He's growing more and more attached to his father. Jackson takes him to the school to shoot basketball on his off days. He reads to him a lot, too. I don't know what Jackson would do without him."

"How's the business going?"

"They just cut the red ribbon yesterday. It will be officially opening tomorrow. You know he named it after him and Tyler?"

"No, I didn't know that."

"We can drive by so you can see it."

"I would like that," Tianna said as she sat back and adjusted her seat.

"I want to see my son first, though."

"He could be with Jackson. Let me call and see."

Tasha spoke into her Bluetooth hands-free link to call "brother."
The phone rang and Jackson picked up after the second ring. Tianna's
heart dropped hearing his voice. It sounded raspy like he was tired. Tasha
asked how he was and how the pharmacy was going, Jackson
acknowledged that it was all good. She handed the conversation over to
Tianna. Jackson hadn't been aware she was in the car.

"How are you, Jackson?"

"I'm cool. You?"

"I miss my son. Can I speak to him? Oh, by the way,
congratulations. I'm proud of you."

"Thanks," he said before he handed the phone to Tyler.

Tyler cleared his voice before he spoke. At times he spoke like an
older child, sometimes like a grown man. Tianna was floored at how
much his voice was changing just over the short span she was gone.

"Hi, Mommy. I miss you. Are you in Texas?"

"Yes, I am. I'm coming by the pharmacy to pick you up so we
can spend some time together."

"Oh, okay. Can Father come too? I want him to be there."

Tianna paused for a minute before she answered. "If Father wants
to."

Tyler turned to Jackson and asked if he wanted to spend time with
him and his mommy.

Jackson didn't know if Tianna had invited him, so he got on the
phone to make sure that it was cool with her.

"Yes, it's fine with me."

"Where are you?"

"We are on our way to see your store."

"Wow, I was just about to lock up. I will wait until you get here."

Tasha and Tianna pulled up in front of the store twenty minutes
later. They got out of the car, looked inside, and saw Tyler and Jackson
playing basketball with the wastebasket and balls of paper. He heard the
tap on the window and saw Tasha and Tianna outside. He hurried to let
them in and locked the door behind him.

"You look and smell nice," Jackson said to Tianna.

"Thank you. And likewise." Tianna smiled.

"Mommy, I missed you!" Tyler said as he ran to hug his mother. She picked him up and gave him one hundred kisses plastered all over his face.

"Mommy, stop it. That's too many kisses. Father, you want some of Mommy's kisses?"

Tianna and Jackson both laughed, but deep down inside, they wanted to kiss each other for all the right and wrong reasons.

Tasha sat back and watched the exchange between her brother, Tianna, and her nephew. She couldn't wait to have her own child and prayed that it would be someday soon. She already had her children's names on speed dial for when she got news of a pregnancy.

She was naming her first son after her father, Adonis. Her little girl would be named Brilliant.

She continued staring at Tianna and wished she could have babies like her without a worry in the world. Tianna smiled back at Tasha. She didn't know what was up with her but would talk to her later.

"Are y'all hungry?" Jackson asked.

"We could eat," Tasha responded.

"I got some cold lunch meat with cheese and crackers in the back."

Tianna shrugged her shoulders and decided to take Jackson up on his offer. Tasha wasn't having it. She wanted a real meal, so she called Darren to see if there were leftovers from the night before and he said that there were. She would be home within thirty minutes. She bid her brother, Tianna, and nephew goodnight. She couldn't wait to get home to her husband.

"Oh, Jackson, before I forget, how many months is Roxanne?" Tasha asked before she left.

"Going on six months. Why?"

"I just asked," Tasha said as she walked out the door. Jackson met her outside to unload Tianna's luggage and put it in his car. Tianna and Tyler went into the back to eat lunch meat and crackers.

Tianna didn't think anything of Tasha's question but when she recalled the airport incident with Roxanne and Markette, she wondered how they knew each other. And most importantly what were they doing together in Texas.

Jackson locked the front door and walked to the back of the store to see Tianna and Tyler eating. He watched them in admiration and thought about how he wanted to officially make them a family. Tyler sat next to Tianna and kept asking her a million questions about her moving to Texas. He didn't want to be away from her. She had one more semester before she would graduate.

"Mommy, are you tired?"

"Why do you ask?"

"Because you keep rubbing your eyes and yawning."

"Yes, it has been a long day."

Jackson asked if she was ready to go home or if she wanted to spend the night with him and Tyler.

Tianna said she couldn't.

"You couldn't or shouldn't?" Jackson asked.

Tianna looked up. Their eyes met and did a familiar dance, one they had been doing since high school. Tianna looked away out the window. Jackson walked close to her and asked what she was thinking about. She was thinking of how she was there with Jackson but in a relationship with Jamal.

"Jackson, there's something I need to tell you."

He let out a sigh, and from the look on Tianna's face, he knew it wasn't good.

"Can whatever you're about to tell me wait? It's a happy day for me and I don't want to ruin it."

"Sure, no problem."

"Father, I'm ready to go home."

"Mommy, are you coming home with Father and me?"

"You can stay in the guestroom. It's yours for however long you need it," Jackson offered.

"Please, Mommy. Stay with Father and me."

Tianna wanted to spend time with her son but she knew that he wanted to stay with his father, so she compromised and accepted the guestroom just for the night.

Tianna excused herself to make a quick phone call to Jamal. She left a message to let him know that she'd made it to Texas and let him know her whereabouts. She told him that she was staying at Tasha's, though in reality she was sleeping over at Jackson's house. She called her mother and grandmother too, to let them know she was staying at Jackson's house.

Bernadette wasn't happy because she knew that Tianna and Jamal were together and that when she was around Jackson, she got sucked in by his charms.

Grandma Debby was ecstatic, she prayed Jackson and Tianna would become a family. She knew how much they loved each other.

Tianna walked inside Jackson's comfy four-bedroom home. He showed her the guestroom and got her fresh towels. Tyler wanted to sleep in the bed with her because he wanted to be near his mother. She gave him his bath and let him stay in the room until he fell asleep and then Jackson carried him to his bedroom and tucked him into bed. He turned on the night light and closed the door.

He walked back to the guestroom and heard the shower running and Tianna singing. He also heard her phone ringing. He looked at the display to see Jamal calling. He didn't know whether to answer it or not. He decided to answer it because he kept calling.

He picked it up and sighed and then pushed the green button.

"Hello, hello?" Jamal kept repeating. He heard Tianna in the background singing and the shower running.

"She's busy right now, call again in the morning," Jackson said and hung up the phone and turned it off.

Jamal kept calling only to hear Tianna's voicemail.

Jackson laid the phone back on the dresser and went to his room. He disrobed and then got into his own shower.

Tianna got out of the shower and put on her nightgown. She slipped into her SpongeBob slippers that she'd had since she was younger and searched for her phone. She found it and noticed that it was turned off. She powered it back on and there were three missed calls from Jamal and angry messages cursing out Jackson.

Tianna was pissed so she went downstairs looking for Jackson, he wasn't downstairs, so she walked back upstairs to look for him. She checked on her son and then entered Jackson's room with a slight knock.

She heard the shower running and decided to wait until he got out so she could give him a heart-to-heart about what he did.

He was taking a little too long in the shower for her liking and she was ready to get some rest, so she knocked on his bathroom door since it was slightly ajar.

"Who is it?" he asked.

He knew exactly who it was and the reason she was there.

"It's me," Tianna answered as she stood at the door.

Without a single warning, Jackson pulled back the shower curtain and there his naked body stood with soap all over it.

Tianna placed her hands over her eyes and yelled, "Jackson."

"What?"

"We need to talk."

"I'm listening," he said with a huge smile across his face as he stood there like a Greek god, water running down every chiseled muscle.

Tianna cleared her throat and turned around so that she could no longer see him. She knew Jackson and his bold attitude.

"Did you answer my phone tonight?"

"Yeah, why?"

"Why did you answer it?"

"Because you were in the shower and it was ringing. Duhhhh." He laughed.

"What did you tell Jamal?"

"I told him the truth, that you were busy, and I let him listen to you showering and singing," he said as he took his shower mitten and applied more body wash to it. "Do you want to join me? Did you get clean enough?"

"Jackson, I'm serious!"

"Me too," he said as he turned off the shower to step out with suds still all over his body.

He walked toward Tianna's backside and she felt his penis and water getting all over her.

He rested his chin on her shoulder and whispered in her ear. "Are you clean enough?"

He took her hands from her face and turned her around. She stood there mesmerized, in a state of shock. She couldn't explain how Jackson controlled her mind and body. It was like he had a remote control where he kept pushing buttons.

He lifted her chin and asked again. "Are you clean enough?"

She looked into his eyes, and in one quick motion, he lifted her up into his arms and her SpongeBob slippers hit the floor. He carried her out of the bathroom and into his bed.

He told Alexa to play "Lose Control" by Silk.

The music began playing and Tianna lost control of her mind, body, and soul. Jackson was the captain of the ship and he was about to go down.

"You still didn't answer me, are you clean enough?"

Her answer was barely audible as Jackson lifted her nightgown and removed her thong with his teeth. Her body was soft like a baby's bottom and she smelled like cherry blossoms. Her scent drove him crazy.

He spread her legs and began moving in a southward direction, caressing her sweet spot. He then devoured her hips, tummy, and finally her tongue.

Tianna's neck arched back and she moaned as she slid her hands down his wet sudsy body. She thought to herself, *What does this man do to me? And why can't I stop him?*

"Jackson, do you have a condom?" she whispered.

He shooed her into silence with his lips as he kissed away her concerns with, "I got you," as he thrust into her like there was no tomorrow and she let him like there was no yesterday.

Her petite fingers grasped for the silk bedsheets and then his body. The music played, and Jackson sang, asking if he could turn her on till the break of dawn.

She didn't answer, so he thrust into her even more. All you could hear were her moans and cries of, "Oh my God, help me." He pleasured her like never before as they both imploded into a world of ecstasy.

Chapter Nineteen

The San Antonio Spurs were leading the New York Knicks at half-time by the score of fifty-eight to fifty-two. Jamal Johnson had fifty percent of the Spurs' points. It had been two weeks since he'd returned from his sprained ankle and he'd picked up where he left off.

Tianna and Tyler sat in the crowd to cheer Jamal on. Tyler had to go to the restroom, so Tianna took him and then got a hot dog and cotton candy on her way back to their courtside seats.

Tyler continued to keep track of Jamal's points. He could count to one-hundred without any hesitation now. His grandmother Sharon was homeschooling him while Jackson worked. Tianna was amazed at how smart he was.

They watched the halftime show and then there was a special announcement made over the PA system. Jamal walked out to the center of the court with a smile on his face.

"Look Mommy, we're on TV," Tyler said as he pointed to the jumbotron.

Tianna looked up and there she and Tyler sat on national TV. She shyly smiled for the camera trying to wrap her mind around what was going on.

She looked at Jamal as he motioned for her to come to him. She pointed at herself and asked, "Me?"

"Yes, you," Jamal motioned as the crowd looked on.

The security guard guided Tianna and Tyler to the center of the basketball court. Tianna's heart beat faster and faster as she walked to center court. Her knees were weak and her hands shook. She held onto Tyler's hand tighter than ever.

"Mommy, are you okay?" Tyler kept asking. But Tianna said nothing. Instead, she kept walking.

She continued to watch the jumbotron as it captured her every move.

She met up with Jamal as he took her hand and got down on one knee. She looked at the jumbotron that read, "Tianna Thompson, will you make me the happiest man by being my wife?"

She covered her mouth and began to cry. She began shaking even more.

She didn't expect what was happening and didn't really have an answer. She loved Jamal with all her heart so she did what a good girl would do. She shook her head and said, "Yes!"

Jamal opened the ring box and placed a three-carat diamond solitaire ring on her finger.

He stood up and kissed her, lifted her up, and spun her around. He was so happy. He got the girl he always wanted. And she said, "YES!"

Tyler began screaming and running around the court as the crowd laughed and cheered.

The announcer congratulated Jamal and Tianna.

Tianna and Tyler walked back to their seats and that is when Tianna's phone began ringing and several text messages flashed through.

Michelle: "Tianna, OMG!!! CONGRATS, BOO!"

Tasha: "Tianna, I know u didn't just accept that proposal. What abt my brother?"

Bernadette: "Congratulations!! I love u!"

Tianna was taken aback by Bernadette's message because her mother had never told her that she loved her. She began to cry. Everything was too overwhelming.

She expected to hear from Jackson, but she didn't. No phone call or text message.

"Mommy, are you okay?" Tyler asked as he began to cry seeing his mother in a state of shock.

Tianna wiped her tears and hugged her son to assure him that her tears were tears of joy.

She sat there admiring her ring and how beautiful it was. She could hardly watch the rest of the game for thinking about Jackson, Jamal, school, Tyler, and her life in general. She had two men that loved her dearly and she didn't want to hurt either of them.

She met Jamal in the Spurs' tunnel, congratulating him on the win and continuing to cry in his arms. He didn't know if she was crying because she was happy or sad, but he it took it as happiness. He was ready to make her his wife and began his family. He played fake boxing with Tyler and told him that he loved him.

"I love you too, Daddy."

"I'll see you in a little bit. Are you going to your mother's or my home?"

"I will be at my mom's," Tianna said.

"Okay, I'll pick you up after our team meeting," he said as he scooped Tianna in his arms for another kiss.

"I love you," he said.

"I love you more."

Markette entered Jackson & Tyler's store. She handed the pharmacist's assistant a prescription for her daughter Emily's ear infection. She sashayed back and forth trying to get Jackson's attention, but he was too distracted by a text message he received from Tasha.

Tasha: "Did u c the Spurs game? Jamal asked Tianna to marry him and she said yes!!!!"

Jackson couldn't believe it, especially after the night he and Tianna had. He just knew he was going to be with her forever. His heart sank. He went from hurt to anger.

He didn't know whether to call her and confirm it, but he knew that Tasha wouldn't lie to him. So, he pulled out his cell phone and typed in ESPN.COM and there it was on the front page: "Jamal Johnson gets the win and engaged." He saw the picture of Jamal kissing Tianna as his son stood by watching.

He rubbed his head in disbelief.

He was glad that the store had only ten minutes until closing. He saw a beautiful white girl waiting for her prescription. He noticed her smiling at him in a flirtatious way. He paid her no mind because his heart belonged to Tianna but she had just broken it. He gave Markette a fake smile in return.

When Emily's prescription was ready, she asked the assistant if she could speak to the pharmacist because she need counseling on her daughter's prescription. The assistant told her to wait and have a seat and she would get the pharmacist.

"Dr. Jackson, we have a client that needs counseling on her daughter's prescription."

"I'll be right there."

Jackson placed his phone in his pocket as it continued to beep with text messages from his parents, Tasha, and one message was from Roxanne.

He walked to the front of the store to counsel Markette about the Amoxicillin. She thanked him and asked for after-hours contact information in case she had further questions. Jackson pulled out his business card that had his cell number and gave it to her.

She took the card and placed it between her lips where her red lipstick made lip imprints, then she placed it inside her bosom and smiled.

She turned and sashayed even more knowing that he was watching.

He watched until she was out of sight.

He walked to the back of the store to turn on his TV and he watched the full engagement of Jamal and Tianna.

His phone beeped with a text message from an unfamiliar number.

Markette: "How about drinks?"

A text message from Roxanne followed:

Roxanne: "Are you okay, baby daddy? I saw the game. I can make u feel better. R"

Jackson closed his phone but not before he responded to Markette's text.

Markette arrived at Jackson's home two hours later. She parked in the driveway next to his car and rang the doorbell. Jackson opened the door and welcomed her inside. He stepped to the left to let her walk past him. He admired her curves. He closed the door and escorted her to the living room while he went into the kitchen to make them drinks.

She took a seat on the sofa. ESPN was on and Jamal and Tianna's engagement kept playing in cycles.

Markette watched with revulsion. She hated Tianna with every inch of her body for what she did to her brother, Mark.

She wanted revenge and she was at Tianna's beloved Jackson's home to seek vengeance.

"So, what did you say your name was?" Jackson asked.

"I didn't, but my name is Mary," Markette said.

Jackson began asking Markette questions about herself and it began to annoy her. She was there to ruin Tianna, not play twenty questions.

"Is this an interview or social time?" she asked as she lifted her glass and drank it down with one shot. Jackson refilled her glass and she continued in this fashion.

She watched SportsCenter and got tired of seeing Tianna's face plastered all over Jackson's eighty-five-inch television set.

"Oh, can you just change the channel? I'm tired of seeing that bitch's face plastered all over television."

Jackson almost spilled his drink when he heard Markette call Tianna a bitch.

"Excuse me? Hold on, do you know her?"

"I don't," Markette stated as Jackson filled her glass for the third time.

He walked to the kitchen to get another bottle of champagne because Markette could really drink. In fact, Jackson was still on his first glass compared to her third. Markette pulled out a tube of Potassium Chloride and mixed it into his drink. Jackson returned and said,

"What did you say your name was?"

"Ummmm, Susan," she said.

"I thought you said 'Mary'?" Jackson said as he watched his drink fizzle up and start to spill over and turn purple.

He put a substance in his drink that would let him know when someone had laced it. Markette watched the drink turn purple as she looked up at Jackson. She picked up the drink and tried to pour it on him. He blocked it with a throw pillow but a little got on his shirt and began to burn. He took off his shirt.

"Lady, I don't know who you are, but it's best for you to leave before I contact the authorities."

Markette thought about Emily and knew that she couldn't afford to go to jail and leave her child with her abusive husband.

She began to profusely apologize to Jackson and offered to leave.

He walked her to the door as she continued to apologize, begging him not to contact the police, explaining that she had a sick child waiting for her at home.

Jackson warned her to never come around him or his store again and she agreed.

He walked her to the door and closed it.

Markette left without another word and sped away in her car while contacting her cousin, Roxanne.

Tianna bathed Tyler and tucked him into bed before she left for Jackson's house. She wanted to explain everything. In fact, last night, their passionate night together wasn't supposed to happen because she was in a relationship with Jamal, and that was what she wanted to talk to him about, but one thing led to another and she found herself in his bed, again.

She called Jackson on his phone but it went straight to voicemail. She called two more times until she finally turned down his street. She pulled up close to his home and saw Markette walking out the door and Jackson without a shirt. She watched Markette speed away.

She killed her headlights and watched Jackson close the door behind her.

Tianna began beating her steering wheel crying. Jackson was back to his old ways and she knew that accepting Jamal's proposal was the right thing to do. She couldn't trust Jackson to keep his penis in his pants.

Not only that, he was screwing Mark's twin sister, Markette! She was so done with him and couldn't wait to get out of Texas.

She hated Jackson.

She loved and hated him all at the same time. She was tired of him breaking her heart but loved the way he made her feel when he wasn't trampling all over her feelings. She loved him with her life.

She sat outside his home for about an hour crying her heart out.

She saw Jackson's front door open and watched him walk toward his trash can with a trash bag in his hand.

Tianna got out of her car and came charging at him.

"You bastard. How could you?" she cried.

"Tianna, what are you doing out here?"

"How could you sleep with Markette?"

"Who's Markette?"

"Don't you play stupid, Jackson. I saw Mark's twin sister leave your home about an hour ago."

"What?"

"I never want to see you ever again, Jackson!"

"Well, good. Because I just saw you get engaged to Jamal on national damn TV! How the hell you think I feel after our night together? Huh?"

"Jackson, don't you dare compare the two of them."

"I won't but I will call it the way I see it. You're here fucking me but getting engaged to another man!"

"I hate you, Jackson!" I hate you!"

"Good, because your ass ain't innocent. Thinking that I'm supposed to wait on you until you make up your goddamn mind!"

"What about Roxanne, your baby's mama? Huh? She ruined my life, our life, with your unborn child! You were supposed to be my first and only, but you go and get someone pregnant? And now I see you with Markette? I hate you, Jackson Jeffrey Norwood!" she cried.

Jackson hated to see her in this position and knew that he'd messed up when he got Roxanne pregnant, but he couldn't do anything about it. What was done was done, but her engagement to Jamal after their night together confused him. He thought that they were going to be a family and work through their relationship with his child from

Roxanne. He loved Tianna and his son, and he wasn't going to give either of them up. They came as a package. But now his family was in the hands of another man.

"Good. Hate me all you want. But you are not innocent, Tianna!"

He kept yelling as she got into her car and drove away.

He walked back toward the house and kicked the trash can. It fell over and the trash fell onto the ground. He picked up the trash and walked into the house.

He knew that Roxanne was a big part of how Tianna was acting, and he didn't blame her, but if he could do it all over again, he would never have slept with Roxanne.

She ruined his relationship with Tianna.

She ruined his life!

Chapter Twenty

Tianna and Michelle sat at the kitchen table planning for the wedding. Tianna hadn't spoken to Tasha in over a month. Every time she called her, she was either busy or asleep. She wanted Tasha to be her maid of honor, but instead she asked Michelle. Michelle was elated, not only to be the maid of honor, but that Tianna was finally through with Jackson. She couldn't stand the way he played with her friend's emotions just because they had a child together. That didn't give him rights to turn her off and on like a light switch.

Michelle was happy to see Tianna and Jamal's relationship getting deeper as the nuptials drew near.

Jamal traveled between Boston and San Antonio whenever he had downtime from the Spurs. He would see his fiancée every chance he got. It was her last semester of school and he wanted her to stay focused because after graduation she was moving back to Texas and he couldn't wait.

He gave Tianna a Black Card and she had unlimited spending to plan the wedding. Whatever she wanted was cool with him.

"What am I going to do without you?" Michelle asked.

"You could move to Texas with me?" Tianna suggested.

"I still have another year left of school."

"I will pay my half of the lease and once you graduate you could move there?"

"What about X?"

"I know. I'm going to miss him, too. I see you two have been getting a little closer. Don't think I didn't notice him leaving your room the other night. So, you need to tell me what's up?"

"Girllll, I'm going to go ahead and tell you. We have been secretly seeing each other since you left for spring break," Michelle confessed as she waved her legs and feet up and down like she was swimming. She was too excited thinking about him.

"Oohhhh, that's what I thought! I knew it!"

"Tianna, I think I'm in love."

"Girl, I know you are in love. Besides, y'all are made for each other. I'm happy for you both. But when were y'all going to tell me?"

"Tell you what?" X said as he entered the room and heard his name.

"Ohhhhhh," Tianna said, as she jumped up to hug him.

"What's that all about?"

"I already know about you," Tianna said.

"What about me?"

"Boy, don't play. I know about you and Michelle!"

X smiled big. He couldn't deny it if he tried. He shook his head and said, "Y'all women gossip too much."

"Whatever, I'm happy for you and Michelle."

X thanked her and then hugged Michelle and gave her a passionate kiss as he walked out the door. He was on his way to save the world.

Michelle thought to herself, *My warrior.*

"Michelle, tell me, is he good in bed?"

"You know I don't kiss and tell. *Unless*, you tell me if Jamal is good in bed."

Tianna looked down because she and Jamal had never had sex, so she couldn't tell her something that she didn't know. Jamal was a virgin and he wanted to wait until marriage before they had sex. He and Tianna had come close to having sex, but he stopped and wanted to wait. She respected his wishes.

It'd been months of only kissing and making out but no intercourse.

She couldn't wait to be Jamal's first and make love to him.

Michelle kept talking but Tianna didn't hear her. She was in a reverie about her soon-to-be husband.

Jackson and Tyler sat at the dining table eating their breakfast before Jackson dropped him off at his parents' home.

"Father, can I call Mommy before we leave?"

"Sure son, let me get my phone."

Jackson walked into his bedroom to unplug his cell phone and walked back into the kitchen.

He gave the phone to Tyler, who began dialing Tianna's number.

Tyler got a message saying that the number had been disconnected and was no longer in service.

"Father, I can't reach her. She's not answering. There's another lady on the phone."

"What do you mean, you can't reach her?"

Jackson took the phone from Tyler and redialed the number. He searched his contact list to find Tianna's number to make sure he was dialing the right one. He got the same message and wondered what was going on.

He contacted Tasha to ask if she had spoken to Tianna. Tasha said that she hadn't but knew that she got a new phone number. She didn't know it.

Tyler began to get cranky because he wanted to call his mother. Jackson explained to him that she got a new phone number and he was trying to get it.

"Oh, that's right. I forgot. I know her new number." Tyler said as he ran to his room to retrieve Tianna's new phone number.
He called and talked to her before he and his father left for the Norwood's home.

They arrived within twenty-five minutes. Sharon was awake waiting for her grandson's arrival. She fixed herself a cup of coffee and looked out the window at the leaves falling. The weather was changing as Autumn was at an end.

She wondered where the years had gone. Her children had moved away and she was grateful she had her grandchild to fill the emptiness of no children in the home.

Adonis was awake, getting ready for his morning run, when he saw Jackson and Tyler pull into the driveway. They walked inside, where he met them.

"Hey son, and good morning, Tyler."

"Good morning, Pops."

"Good morning, Grandpa."

"Hi Tyler, come give Grandma a hug." Sharon extended her arms to wrap them around her only grandchild.

"Jackson, do you have a minute? I want to talk to you."

"Sure. What's up?"

"So, how are you?"

"Things are going well. Business is good. Everything is cool."

"Naw, I'm talking about how are you, really?"

"What are you getting at?" Jackson asked.

"I'm talking about your love life, son."

Jackson chuckled because his father had never asked about his love life before. He didn't know if he was asking how many women he had bedded since Tianna or what. The answer was zero, but he knew as a man he couldn't say that he wasn't getting any. So instead, he said,

"It's complicated."

"Yeah, I know, son. How many months is Roxanne?"

"She's at the end of her eighth month."

"When is the next doctor visit?"

"It's next week. Pop, why all these questions? You got something to say?"

"Yeah, I got a lot to say, but I don't know if it's my place or not."

Jackson wanted his father's advice. He needed it more than ever, and in fact, welcomed it. He knew that something was weighing heavy on his heart because this was the first time he asked about Roxanne and his unborn grandchild.

Adonis talked about women and how complicated they could be. He told him about how manipulating some were and how you had to sleep with one eye open and one eye closed until you found the right one. He asked Jackson if he had any feelings for Roxanne, and Jackson immediately said no. He got involved with a woman that he didn't love and a child he hadn't bonded with. He felt bad saying that about his child, but it was the truth.

He talked about how he only saw Roxanne to take her to the monthly appointments and once they heard the baby's heartbeat and that she was doing well, he'd leave.

He confessed his love for Tianna. He said that he wasn't over her and hadn't moved on. He tried, but he found it difficult. Every time he looked at his son, he saw Tianna. Every time he saw Roxanne, he was reminded of how she destroyed his relationship with Tianna.

He knew that she was getting married soon and the closer it got to the day, the more depressed he became.

His father talked about how he never gave up or quit on things that he wanted in life. He used his education and his business as an example.

"Why are you giving up on Tianna?"

"I'm not, but she's in love with Jamal."

"You know she ain't a bit or more in love with Jamal than a man on a moon. I've watched Tianna grow from a little girl into a woman. She looks at you the same way your mother used to look at me."

"Dad, Tianna has moved on. She doesn't want me. She hates me."

"Son, that's nonsense! Tianna loves you. And I didn't raise you to be no quitter."

"Thanks, Dad," Jackson said as he gave his father a hug and got into his car to drive to work. He pushed play on his playlist and "The Reasons" serenaded through his speakers.

He pulled up to the front of his store and looked at his cell phone. He checked the last number that was dialed by Tyler and saved it to his contact list under Tianna's name. It still had her and his son's picture with emoji hearts next to it. He looked at her face and smiled.

There was a knock at Roxanne's door. She looked through the peephole and saw Ruby standing there in tears. She couldn't believe it. She opened the door immediately before anyone could see her.

"Oh my God, what's wrong?"

"I've been spotting all night and I can't feel the baby move."

"Did you call the doctor?"

"No, I wanted to let you know first. I called but you didn't answer."

"Okay, we need to get you into the hospital quick, but we're going to go to another hospital that's not close by."

Roxanne got dressed and she and Ruby parked in the parking lot of University Hospital.

Ruby became weaker and weaker as she continued to lose large amounts of blood.

Roxanne was not only worried about her sister's health but losing Jackson in the process. Her entire life was in the hands of Ruby's unborn child.

Ruby was admitted by Nurse Williams. She called Shantae into the room to help her with Ruby because she was losing so much blood she could hardly walk.

Shantae got a wheelchair and took her down to the critical care unit while Nurse Williams contacted Dr. Anderson.

Nurse Williams assisted Ruby in disrobing and getting her into a gown for observation. She took her vitals and began an IV on her. She instructed Shantae to talk to Roxanne and get as much information as possible to find out what was causing the bleeding.

Nurse Williams worked fast, getting Ruby situated to do a sonogram and check on the child.

Meanwhile, Shantae got a chart and documented personal information as well as medical history.

"Who is the father of the child?" Shantae asked.

"His name is Jackson Norwood, but he doesn't want nothing to do with her."

"Excuse me. Did you say Jackson Norwood?"

"Yeah, that's what I said. Jackson Jeffrey Norwood to be exact."

Shantae dropped her pen along with the chart. She'd just seen Jackson eight months ago with Tasha and Tianna. *Could this be the woman that drugged him?* Shantae thought to herself.

"And what is your name, Ms.?"

"I'm Roxanne, Ruby's twin sister."

So, this is the woman that drugged Jackson. Shantae excused her clumsiness, picked up her pen and chart, and kept writing all the information Roxanne gave about Ruby.

"Can you please hurry this up? I have to check on my baby—I mean, sister."

Shantae couldn't believe her ears. She didn't know that what she was hearing was supposed to be confidential, and if it was to get out, it could mean life and death for all parties involved.

"Sure, one more question and we should be done. Would you like to contact the father of the child to let him know that your sister is here?"

"No, absolutely not! Under no circumstances should you contact Jackson Norwood!"

Tasha waited anxiously for the results of her and Darren's fertility treatments. She couldn't stop worrying about her future without children.

"Tasha, I don't like to see you like this, baby. If we can't have children of our own, then we will adopt. It's really a win-win situation."

"I want to experience motherhood. I want my daughter and son to look like me or you. It's not a win-win. I want to bear my own children." She cried into her husband's arms.

He held her tight and silently prayed that they could have children of their own.

She had been depressed for months about not being able to conceive. She isolated herself from friends and family and only came around sporadically or checked in enough for them not to worry.

She did talk to Jackson often because he filled her prescription every month. But each time she came by Jackson & Tyler pharmacy, she looked more and more depressed.

Jackson tried his best to breathe life into her situation and kept positively reinforcing to her that it would happen.

Dr. Watson entered the room to give Tasha and Darren the good news that her body was responding to the medication and that it was just a matter of time.

"Oh, thank you, Dr. Watson. I couldn't bear to hear any bad news. This has really taken a toll on me lately."

He advised her to worry less because it was hampering her chances of conceiving. He promised her that it would happen soon, *real* soon.

Chapter Twenty-One

Graduation day was one week away. Tianna had completed her law degree and was graduating at the top of her class. Jamal was expected to fly in tonight to help put the final touches on their wedding plans. Even though he gave Tianna the green light to do whatever she wanted at his expense, she still sought his opinions.

"Hey babe, what time does your flight arrive?"
"It should be in Boston no later than three p.m."
"Okay. That gives me time to check on a few things before coming to pick you up."
"I love you," Jamal crooned into the phone.
"I love you more," Tianna cooed back.
When Tianna hung up the phone, she saw Michelle on her way out the door. She stopped her to ask if she wanted to go with her to pick up her wedding dress and the bridesmaid dresses, and she would take her out to eat afterwards. She had to meet the wedding planner at Jacqueline's Bridal Shop within an hour.
Michelle wasn't the type to turn down a free meal, and she wanted to see her dress as well, so she asked if they could stop and give X the paperwork he left at home, and then she would gladly be her guest.
Tianna grabbed her purse, locked the door, and set the alarm as she and Michelle stopped at X's office space. They pulled up in Tianna's candy apple BMW that attracted a lot of attention because of its custom designs.
Michelle got out of the car and there was a crowd of about ten people standing there holding protest signs. One sign read: *Black American Justice. When the murdered are on trial for their own murder!!*
Michelle read the sign and said,
"I know that's right!"
She asked Tianna if she wanted to come inside with her and said she would only be inside for a minute.
Tianna looked at the crowd standing there and decided to wait in the car.

"Okay, suit yourself," Michelle said as she walked into the building searching for X.

She found him and he embraced her with a hug and kiss.

"I'm with Tianna. We are going to pick up our dresses and then going out to eat. Do you need anything else?" she asked as she handed him the paperwork.

"Naww. I'm good. Are you and Tianna coming out to the rally tonight?"

"I don't know if Tianna is because Jamal is coming into town, so she might want to spend time with him, but I will be there," she assured him.

"Yeah, she ain't coming out tonight. All right, I will see you later. Appreciate you."

"You better," Michelle teased as she kissed him and walked away.

He watched her until she was out of sight. *Man, I love that woman*, he thought to himself.

When Michelle opened the door to get to Tianna's car, one of the patrons told her, "You know you are about to marry the next Malcolm X?"

She laughed and told the lady, "No, I'm about to marry the next President of the United States."

"Oh, sho you're right!" the lady said as she gestured in an upward motion meaning, "yes."

Michelle got into Tianna's car and they drove to Jacqueline's Bridal Shop. The shop was crowded with soon-to-be brides and relatives trying on dresses and getting fitted.

"Oh, Ms. Thompson. Right this way, please," said Tina, the wedding planner, as soon as she saw Tianna and Michelle.

They followed her to the back of the store and into a dressing room where her white floral gown hung with a three-foot train. It was even more beautiful than before she'd had it altered.

"Tianna, let's go ahead and try it on to make sure everything fits to perfection. Michelle, you can use this room to try yours on as well."

Michelle was the first to come out and spin around in her dress. She looked beautiful, as her dress accented her small curvy waistline. She kept looking in the mirror and taking silly selfies so she could post them on Facebook.

Michelle noticed that Tianna was taking forever to come out. So, she called, "Tianna, do you need any help getting into your dress?"

At first she didn't answer because she was too busy trying to figure out why her dress was no longer fitting her.

"No, I'm fine. Just give me a minute," she assured Tina and Michelle.

Michelle took a few more selfies before she went back into the dressing room to take off her dress and place it in the plastic wrap. When she came back, Tianna was still in the room and hadn't come out.

"Tianna, what are you doing? You're not getting cold feet, are you?" Michelle giggled.

"Yeah, Tianna, let's see how beautiful you look in your dress," Tina said.

"I'll be out in a minute."

"I'm giving you one minute. If you are not out in a minute then I'm coming in," Michelle threatened.

The door opened and Tianna stood there with the dress snuggled tightly on her tummy. She couldn't get the dress zipped up even with Tina and Michelle's help.

"What the hell?" Michelle said aloud.

"I know I got the right measurements down," Tina assured her.

"Damn, how much weight did you gain in two months?"

"I don't know," said Tianna.

"The wedding is still one month away. We can have it altered again with no problem," Tina said.

"Tina, I'm so sorry. Would it be a problem for you? I know you have other clients."

"Trust me, Tianna. This happens all the time and it's the reason I ask my clients to try on their dresses before leaving.

"Okay. I will take the dresses and have my bridesmaids try theirs on to make sure they still fit."

"That would be great," Tina said.

Tianna handed her the Black Card, paying for all the dresses, including her own that still needed to be altered.

Tianna and Michelle left the bridal shop and decided to go to the mall and pick up their shoes and accessories. After getting their shoes, they both were starving.

"What do you want to eat?" Tianna asked.

"I don't know, but anywhere is fine with me as long as it's a place that has good salads."

"Since when do you eat salads?" Tianna asked.

"Oh, I don't. It's not for me, it's for you," Michelle teased.

Tianna decided to drive outside of the mall and eat at Saltgrass Steakhouse. She had the chicken salad with olive oil and Michelle ate smothered steak with gravy, mashed potatoes, and green beans.

Michelle kept licking her fingers and making all kinds of moans at how good the food was. She only did it to tease Tianna. Tianna laughed and called Michelle a fool. After they finished eating, Tianna dropped Michelle off at X's office space while she went to the airport to pick up Jamal.

Tianna arrived thirty minutes before Jamal's plane was scheduled to land. She found parking and hurried inside the airport. She sat down in her seat and decided to call Tyler to check on him. She reached into her purse and noticed Markette sitting in a chair with her daughter, Emily. A few minutes later, she noticed Roxanne handing Markette a Mountain Dew. Tianna watched Roxanne and Markette's every move. Markette noticed Tianna staring at her but she looked away. It was strange for Markette to turn away from Tianna as if she'd seen a ghost. Whenever Markette had encountered Tianna in the past her form of communication was an eye roll and sucking her teeth. This time it was a discreet movement as she continued holding her daughter in her arms.

Roxanne sat next to Markette checking her phone every five minutes like she was waiting on an important phone call.

An announcement was made indicating that Jamal's flight had arrived and Tianna stood up to locate him. She looked directly at Roxanne as she shifted to adjust her overcoat.

Tianna stared right at her tummy and then looked away. She despised Roxanne. She'd played a big role in her and Jackson not being together. She also felt that an outside child had ruined her life with the man she loved.

Markette usually had something smart to say about Tianna, but this time she barely looked her way. She just kept attending to her daughter.

Jamal located Tianna before she saw him. He came from behind her and kissed her on the back of her neck. She knew it was him because she knew his cologne. She turned around and gave him a big smile and embrace.

"I've missed you so much," he said, holding her in his arms.

"I know. I couldn't wait to see you."

"Excuse me, Mr. Jamal, can I please have your autograph?" A little boy wearing Jamal's jersey stood there with a Spurs game book in his hand, holding it out to Jamal.

Jamal smiled and not only gave the little boy his autograph but took a selfie with him and his relative that was with him at the airport. He has never turned anyone away for selfies or autographs.

A few more patrons came up to Jamal and Tianna before they left to get into the car.

"That's why I love you so much. You never let your fame change who you have always been," "Naw, that's one of the promises I made to myself is to never get so big that I don't remember how I was as a kid and wanted a lot of these stars' autographs but never got them."

Jamal placed his luggage in the trunk.

He sat on the passenger's side of the car and Tianna drove off. She began telling him about her day and how the wedding dress didn't fit and that she had to get it altered again, but for him not to worry that it would be ready in time. She told him about graduation day and how she invited family and friends from Texas. Jamal wanted to ask if Jackson was invited but decided against it because he was Tyler's father. Besides, she was marrying him, not Jackson, so it was all good if he was invited.

"I went by to see Tyler the other day. Man, he's getting so big. It seems like I'm missing out on his life," Jamal said as he looked out the window watching the wintry mix of winter coming soon.

"Well, he's five years old now. I've missed him dearly, but graduation is next week, and once it's over I will be moving back to Texas planning our wedding. I will never miss another day of his life."

"I'm grateful to still have him in my life and that Jackson didn't completely take him away. I went to see him on his birthday before he and Jackson took off to Disneyland."

Tianna smiled as if to say she was proud of Jackson too, that he didn't object to Tyler calling Jamal "Daddy." Jackson was being mature about the whole situation.

"Are you hungry?" Tianna asked.

"I can eat. You?"

"Michelle and I just ate a few hours before I picked you up. I need to watch my weight so that I'll be able to fit into my dress."

"Beautiful, don't worry about your weight. If you can't fit into it then we will just get you another dress. I want you to be happy."

Tianna reached for Jamal's hand and told him that she was happy.

He placed a sincere kiss on her hand. A kiss of endearment. They were in love and soon she would be Tianna Johnson. *His* wife.

Chapter Twenty-Two

Jackson dialed Roxanne's number for the fifth time. He was
waiting outside the doctor's office for her to arrive for her monthly
checkup. She was always on time and he wondered if something had
happened. He didn't know any of her family, so he didn't know who to
contact to check on her.
He decided to wait for another thirty minutes before he took off to her
apartment.

Jackson arrived at Roxanne's condo within twenty-five minutes.
He'd just missed her. She was on her way to visit her sister Ruby in the
hospital after she dropped Markette off at the airport.

He pulled out his phone to call her again but there was no answer.
It went straight to voicemail.

He hung up and decided to drive to work.

When he pulled up in the driveway of Jackson & Tyler pharmacy,
he saw Shantae entering his store.

He thought to himself, *What is she doing here?* He didn't have
time for her or anything she had to say.

He got out of the car and opened the door to the pharmacy. He
heard Shantae asking his assistant for him and her telling Shantae that he
wasn't in. The assistant saw Jackson enter and said,

"Oh, there's Dr. Norwood."

Shantae turned around and smiled when she saw Jackson walking
toward them with a white lab coat and stethoscope wrapped around his
neck. Most pharmacists didn't wear stethoscopes, but Jackson did
because he often manually took patients' vitals.

Shantae walked toward Jackson and said that she needed to talk to
him and that it was very important.

"I don't have time for your games, Shantae."

"Jackson, trust me. It's not a game. It's about Roxanne Carter."

Jackson heard Roxanne's name and knew that it was serious
because Shantae didn't know Roxanne, or he thought she didn't.

Jackson took Shantae to his personal office and closed the door.

She told him about her encounter at the hospital with Roxanne, and her twin sister Ruby's pregnancy. She swore him to confidentiality since she would be violating the HIPPA law. He took the oath and she began singing like a canary.

Jackson couldn't believe his ears. He had been played by Roxanne. He fell for the okie-doke.

The bait and switch. The lie.

He and Shantae talked for about fifteen minutes in privacy. He walked her to the front door and gave her a hug and thanked her.

Tianna had just hung up the phone with Tasha when Jamal entered the room. Tasha was going to be a part of her wedding and she and Darren would be attending her graduation. The Norwoods were coming down along with her mother and grandmother. Her deceased father Tyrone's mother, Terrie, would also be attending. She didn't ask about Jackson, although she wanted him there, but then again, she didn't. She didn't want to deal with his antics and the unexplainable control he had over her emotions. She was marrying Jamal despite, or *in* spite of Jackson.

"Hey Jamal, I didn't hear you come in. I was going to ask if you could pick up my mother, Tyler, and grandma up from the airport tonight? I have to get my hair done and we have to rehearse for graduation day."

"I got you, Tianna. I will handle it all. I just want you to take it easy. You have a lot going on. You've been throwing up and I just want you to get some rest."

Tianna was shocked when she heard Jamal say that she had been throwing up. She had a little morning sickness but it wasn't a big deal. She sometimes felt queasy after she had eaten something she didn't agree with. She also wondered if Jamal felt left out since she had so much to do and very little time was spent with him.

"Jamal, I'm fine. It's just a lot going on with graduation and the wedding. I'm sorry if you feel left out. It's not my intent. Besides, we have the rest of our lives together," she said as she batted her dark beaded eyes and kissed him. "I love you so much."

He returned her love by cupping her chin and laying a passionate kiss on her lips. They began making out.

There was a knock on the door that neither of them heard. The knock got louder as the door opened into the bedroom.

"All right, you two lovebirds, the wedding is weeks away. Y'all can wait," Michelle said.

"Hey Michelle, what are you up to?"

"Nothing, I needed to talk to you about something."

"Sure."

Jamal stood there with Tianna waiting for Michelle to talk but she looked at him as if to say, "Alone, without you." So, Jamal pointed to himself and asked if she wanted him to leave and Michelle said, "Please. I won't be too long with your soon-to-be wife." She giggled.

Jamal and Tianna gave each other one last embrace before he left the room.

"Jackson called for you on the main landline when you were out. He said that he had something important to tell you."

Tianna sighed, she didn't have time for Jackson and whatever he had to tell her. It was over between them and she was marrying Jamal and there was nothing or no one getting in the way, not even Jackson.

"Michelle, if he calls again, please just take a message. Unless it's something about Tyler."

"I got you, girl. I wish you would let me tell him a piece of my mind."

"Thanks, Michelle, but that won't be necessary."

Tianna and Michelle talked about graduation and what she was going to wear. Michelle wanted Tianna's opinion about her dress and hairdo. Tianna suggested that they go and get their hair and make-up done together.

She and Jamal were having a private dinner at a fancy restaurant he reserved. So, getting her hair and make-up done would be perfect timing.

She called Jamal back into the room and they made-out a little more before he left to pick up her parents and Tyler at the airport.

After talking with Shantae, Jackson called Roxanne again, but to no avail. He went by her job after work to see if she was there but Stephen said she hadn't been to work in over a week. He had warned Jackson that something was up with Roxanne a long time ago and that she couldn't be trusted.

Jackson waited and waited outside her apartment all night. Tyler was with Tianna's mother and grandmother, and they were on their way to Boston to see Tianna graduate. His parents and Tasha were going too. Jackson had been planning to attend, but when Shantae told him about Roxanne he stayed in Texas to get to the end of her lies.

It was around midnight when he saw Roxanne pull up into the parking garage of the condo. He got out of his car and silently walked up behind her until she got to her front door and opened it.

"Where have you been?" he asked, scaring the living daylights out of her.

"Jackson, w-what are you doing here?" she stuttered, trying to put on a straight face.

"I asked you a question. Where have you been? And why weren't you at the doctor's office today?"

"I was, it's just that I was running late."

"Why didn't you call and let me know? I was there waiting for you for over an hour."

"Ummmm, I don't know. I guess it just slipped my mind," she said as she continued to walk inside her apartment. Jackson walked in behind her, leaving her no room to breathe.

"So, how is my baby?" he asked as he opened Roxanne's coat to see her stomach.

"The baby is fine." She pushed his hands away from her stomach.

"I want to see her."

"Jackson, there's nothing to see. You know she isn't born yet."

"I know. I want to rub your stomach."

"Jackson, I'm tired, and I'm sure the baby is too. Can you come back tomorrow? I need to get some rest. It's been a long day."

Jackson was no longer falling for her lies, so he ripped open her blouse and that's where he saw an artificial baby bump. He ripped off her bra to see the left side of her breast and there was the birthmark that he never saw on her when they were at the doctor's office.

"What is this?"

"Jackson, I can explain," she cried out.

"Yeah, you *better* start explaining."

Roxanne asked him to have a seat and he reluctantly took it. She talked about her cousin Mark, and how he had paid her to ruin Tianna and Jackson's lives. He wanted to destroy Tianna for cheating on him. She told him she was never pregnant, but her sister Ruby was, and that she was in the hospital with complications. It was Ruby that was going to the doctor's appointments with him. She explained that she didn't want to go through with the plan after she'd met and fallen in love with him, but it was too late.

She told him that Markette was in Texas to make sure that the plan was going according to Mark's instructions. But Mark was impatient, and he'd sent Markette to kill him by putting poison in his drink.

Jackson thought over everything Roxanne was saying. He'd seen that there was no birthmark on Ruby's left breast but hadn't questioned it. He remembered how he'd bumped into Ruby when she was at the restaurant shortly after Roxanne spiked his drink. He never knew she had a twin. In fact, he never knew anything about Roxanne. He'd just wanted a piece of ass to get over Tianna, and she had been available.

It was Markette trying to poison him that took him over the top. He couldn't believe what a crazy family Tianna had gotten mixed up with. He wanted to go file charges, but Roxanne begged him not to and promised that he would never hear from her again.

She apologized profusely for her part in attempting to ruin his life. She cried and asked for forgiveness. She hoped it wasn't too late for him to get Tianna back and told him that she'd seen Tianna and Jamal at the airport. She loved Jackson and wanted him to be happy, so she told him to go get Tianna because he was the one for her, not Jamal. Tianna loved him.

Jackson thought about it for a minute and looked at his watch. He wanted to catch the next flight out to Boston. He had to get Tianna back. He had to tell her that there was no baby.

She couldn't marry Jamal. He had to stop the wedding.

Tasha and Darren sat in the doctor's office waiting to hear the results of her third pregnancy test.

She had taken two home pregnancy tests that showed she was pregnant. She and Darren were so excited that they wanted to make sure before they told the family.

They sat holding hands and Darren hugged his wife and softly stroked her right shoulder while she rested her head on him.

She couldn't wait to tell her parents that they were having another grandbaby. She didn't care about the sex of the child as long as it was healthy. She thought about how she was going to be a good mother like her mom and see to it that the child received a good education. She had her future planned, she just wanted to hear the results from the doctor.

Tasha and Darren were called to the back and were elated when they saw Dr. Watson walk out with a smile. They smiled back.

"Congratulations, you're going to be parents."

Tasha cried in her husband's arms. He cried, too. This was the happiest day of their lives. It was finally happening. She was going to be a mother.

She couldn't wait to tell her parents.

Chapter Twenty-Three

Graduation day was over and Tianna was a Harvard graduate.

She had returned home to marry Jamal. She couldn't wait to be his wife and continued planning her future with him in Texas. She was finally home.
She'd spoken to Tasha earlier and heard about Tasha's pregnancy. She was going to be the godmother of her and Darren's unborn child.

Tianna was missing Michelle, but she and X would be there in two days for the wedding.
She felt sick and didn't know how much longer she could go with limited sleep. She was exhausted and her body was letting her know. She continued throwing up each morning and felt nauseated throughout the day.
"Tianna, are you okay?" Grandma Debby stood outside Tianna's bedroom door. She'd heard her throwing up repeatedly.
"Granny, I'm okay. I just ate something that didn't agree with me."
Debby thought this had been happening since Tianna returned home. She'd also noticed at dinner the night before that she hardly ate anything.
"All right. I just wanted you to know that Jackson just left. Bernadette told him that you weren't here. You need to talk to him. He has been coming by every day looking for you.
"Granny, Jackson has a child on the way. He needs to go visit his baby mama."
"Well, aren't you his 'baby mama'?"
"Granny, I'm talking about Roxanne."
"Nonsense, that boy ain't a bit worried about that baby mama," Debby said as she closed Tianna's bedroom door.
After Debby left, Tyler came into the room to check on his mother and to ask if he could go to Grandpa Adonis's house. He and his grandpa were building a treehouse and he wanted to continue it before it rained over the weekend.
"Mommy, can you take me to my Papa's house?"

"Let mommy get dressed and I will take you."

Tyler cheered and ran out the bedroom. He got on the phone and called his grandparents to let them know that he was on his way. He also called his father and told him his plans.

Tianna walked out of the restroom and saw Tyler on her phone.

"Who were you talking to?"

"I was talking to my papa and Father."

Tianna didn't want to talk to Jackson and didn't want him to know her whereabouts, but she couldn't let her son know that she was avoiding his father like the plague.

"You got your backpack and things ready?"

"Yes, Mommy. I got everything."

Tianna left to drop Tyler at the Norwoods. She also wanted to stop at the store to get a pregnancy test. She knew that she wasn't pregnant, but she couldn't explain why she kept feeling queasy all day and night.

She exchanged pleasantries with the Norwoods and they talked about the wedding two days away. She bid her son goodbye and she was off to the store.

She walked inside Rite Aid and found the pregnancy tests. She chose the First Response brand. As she read the instructions, she quickly walked to the cash register to pay without anyone noticing her.

As she walked out of the store she bumped into Darren, her bag dropped, and the pregnancy test fell out of the bag.

"Hey Tianna, I'm sorry. I didn't know you were already in town. I thought you were due in later tonight?" Darren said as he picked up Tianna's bag and pretended like he didn't see what was inside.

"Oh, hey, Darren. I just got into town. Ummm, how are you?"

"I'm good. I know Tasha told you the good news about the baby."

"Yes, she did. And congratulations. I'm so happy for you."

"Are you ready for the big day?"

Tianna smiled and assured Darren that she was ready to marry Jamal and talked about how much she loved him. She asked him what he was doing at the store and he told her about the software program he was selling and installing. He didn't ask her about her visit because he'd seen the pregnancy test.

They continued to talk but Tianna had to cut it short to go pick up her dress. She was meeting with the wedding planner.

She hurried home, went into her bathroom, and locked the door.

She continued reading the instructions on the pregnancy test. She heard her phone ring but ignored it.

She opened the test and pulled out a paper cup she had from the cup dispenser. She pulled her pants down and cleaned her vagina with a sanitary wipe before she peed into the cup. She dipped the pregnancy stick inside the warm urine and waited for a few seconds before reading the results.

Her phone continued to ring and ring. She pulled up her pants, washed her hands, and rushed out to retrieve her phone.

"Hello," Tianna answered.

"Hey girl, I'm at the airport with X and our ride hasn't shown up. Can you please come get us? We've been here for hours."

"Oh yes, sure. I'm on my way right now," Tianna said as she rushed out the door and told her mother she was on her way to the airport to pick up Michelle and X and she had to meet with the wedding planner, too.

As she drove off, she passed Jamal. He was on his way to see her and go over their wedding plans. She didn't notice him, she was in such a hurry. She didn't even read the pregnancy results before she left.

Jamal didn't bother going after her. He would just go to her mother's house and wait until she returned. He wanted to get a little rest as well.

He parked his truck and rang the doorbell. Bernadette answered and told him that Tianna went to the airport. He knew she was in a hurry but didn't know why. He asked Bernadette if he could go up to Tianna's room and wait for her and get a little rest. She was more than thrilled to have Jamal around. So, it was fine with her. She let him in.

He walked up to Tianna's room and laid on her bed. He saw the bag from Rite Aid and looked inside to see the receipt. He read the receipt and saw that she'd purchased a pregnancy test. He walked into her private restroom and saw the pregnancy test stick on the counter. He got closer and picked up the stick to read the results.

He placed the stick back where he found it and walked down the stairs to leave.

"Hey Jamal, I thought you were going to wait for Tianna?" Bernadette said.

"You know, I forgot I had to take care of something, so I will be back. Could you not tell Tianna that I was here?"

"Ummm, okay. Whatever you say." She wanted to ask why but decided not to.

She looked at Debby and shrugged her shoulders.

Jackson waited and waited outside Tianna's house, but she never came home. *She must be with Jamal*, he thought. His heart was so broken that he didn't know what to do. Tianna was marrying Jamal the next day and he had less than ten hours to convince her not to.

He dialed Tianna's number and it went straight to her voicemail. He left over twenty messages. He was like a mad man.

Earlier in the day, he'd spoken to his parents again and told them everything that had happened with Roxanne. Sharon was so upset. She knew that her son was distraught about Tianna marrying Jamal and that he really loved her. She wanted to give Roxanne a piece of her mind. She'd ruined Jackson and Tianna's relationship with her lies.

Jackson wasn't giving Tianna up so easily. He went into his old room and saw the poster board that he'd made in high school asking Tianna to go to the prom with him. He'd been too scared to ask her and had stuck the poster board back in his closet. He sat on his bed reminiscing about her and the day she'd first caught his attention with a denim outfit she wore at a basketball game. He cried and laughed. She was getting married tomorrow.

He drove home with the poster board in hand. He went to his bedroom, had a few drinks, and turned the TV on SportsCenter. The analysts talked about Jamal's big wedding day.

He saw pictures of Jamal and Tianna looking happily in love.

He drank and cried himself to sleep.

The church was filled with friends and family along with a lot of NBA players and their wives. There were news cameras everywhere. It seemed like Jamal was having a royal wedding.

Flowers and a big waterfall stood in the center of the church as guests continued to pack inside.

Everyone was waiting for the bride and groom to arrive.

Jamal arrived first with Darren by his side. They went to the back room to get dressed and put the final touches on their tuxedos.

"Hey Jamal, are you ready?"

"Man, I've never been readier in my life. I've loved Tianna for as long as I've known her. Yes, I'm ready."

They gave each other a brotherly hug as X walked into the room to inform Jamal that Tianna had arrived. Jamal's heart began beating faster and faster. He hadn't been sure she would show up. He thought that maybe she would get cold feet, but no, she was there to marry him.

He smiled inside and out.

Tianna, Michelle, Tasha, and the other bridesmaids were getting dressed. They had just returned from getting their hair and make-up done. The final dress rehearsal was here, meaning the real wedding.

Tianna asked about Tyler and his whereabouts. He was with Sharon and Adonis so she didn't have to worry. She got word that Jamal was there, and it was only a matter of minutes before she walked down the aisle to him. She hadn't seen him in almost two days, since he passed her on her way to the airport. After picking up X and Michelle she dropped them off at the Sheraton hotel and rushed home to see the result of her test.

Adonis was giving Tianna away since she was like a daughter to him. Tianna missed her father and wished he was there to give her away.

There was a knock on the door. It was Bernadette coming to check on her daughter to see if she needed anything. She had tears in her eyes because she was so proud of her. She'd graduated from Harvard University and now she was getting married. It was like a dream come true for Bernadette, except it was Tianna's reality.

"Tianna, I just want you to know how proud I am of you. You are much more than I could have ever expected."

"Mama, don't cry. You're going to make me cry. I can't cry because I don't want to ruin my make-up."

She embraced her mother and Bernadette left to take her seat in the church.

There was another tap at the door letting Tianna know that it was time for her to make her entrance.

"T, you ready?" Tasha asked.

Tianna nodded yes. Michelle said, "Let's do this," as all the bridesmaids followed.

Tyler stood at the doorway of the church with Adonis as they waited for Tianna. When Tyler saw his mother he yelled, "Mommy, you look so beautiful!"

The church erupted in laughter as the piano began to play "Here Comes the Bride."

Adonis held his hand out and Tianna placed her hand in his and held it tight. She mouthed "thank you." He kissed her softly on her forehead.

As Tianna walked down the aisle, she saw Jamal standing in his black tuxedo and turquoise shirt, his hair freshly cut and trimmed, his goatee nicely shaped. His smile could cure cancer, that's how potent it was. She looked at her Grandma Debby and she had tears in her eyes.

Tianna walked and met Jamal at the altar.

"Hey beautiful," he said.

Tianna trembled inside and out as she mouthed, "hey" to Jamal.

They turned to the reverend and he began the nuptials.

"Dearly beloved, we are gathered here today…"

When the reverend finished announcing Tianna and Jamal's names, music came over the sound system. It was a familiar tune, but Tianna and the patrons looked around.

"Let me know" by Aaliyah serenaded the entire church.

People began to shift around and talk, trying to find out where the music was coming from. And there he stood at the entrance of the church walking inside with the poster board he made in high school that read: **"Will you go to prom with me?"** But he had added to it: **"Will you go to prom with me and marry me?"**

Jackson stood at the center of the church walking down the aisle holding the poster board.

Tianna looked at Jackson as their song continued playing in the background. She turned toward her mother and grandmother and Debby nodded her head, "yes."

Adonis smiled big and his chest puffed out thinking, *There's my son. He never quits.*

The closer Jackson walked to Tianna the more tears ran down her face. She looked at Jamal and he looked shocked and confused. She looked between Jackson and Jamal the closer he got to them.

It looked like Tianna was playing, "Eeny, meeny, miny, moe" the way she looked between the two, and said, "I'm sorry."

Jamal took Tianna in his arms and whispered to her, "It's okay, beautiful. I will always love you."

Jamal took Tianna's hand and placed it in Jackson's.

She looked at Jackson and he said, "I love you, Tianna, can we please talk?"

Jamal told her to go with Jackson in the back so they could talk. The cameras flashed and patrons began to talk in disbelief wondering who Jackson was and what was going on?

The reverend asked everyone to calm down and remain seated until further notice. Tianna walked with Jackson to the back room.

"Jackson, what are you doing?"

"I'm coming to get *my* woman. I came to marry you."

"What about Roxanne and your baby?"

"She lied, there is no baby. That's what I've been calling trying to tell you. Roxanne is Mark's cousin and he sent her to ruin our relationship. There was never no baby."

Tianna couldn't believe the measures that Mark had gone through to ruin her. But she didn't want to talk about him on her wedding day. Instead, she was happy to hear that Jackson didn't have a child aside from Tyler, so she told him another one of her secrets.

"Jackson, I'm pregnant."

"I don't care. I love you, Tianna. We can make it work. Besides, Jamal isn't a bad dude. I can accept his child."

"Jackson, it's not Jamal's baby."

"Tianna, I don't care whose baby it is, *I love you.*"

He kept saying this without letting her get a word in.

"Jackson, listen to me." She palmed his face with her hands. "It's your baby!"

"What?"

"Yes, it's *your* baby."

He took Tianna in his arms and yelled, "It's my baby?! It's my baby?" he kept asking and cupping her stomach. Tianna kept assuring him that it was.

They kissed and embraced, and he showed her the poster board he made when he was in high school. But he was too afraid to ask her to the prom. She laughed and thought it was so cute.
He asked if she would go to the prom and marry him? And she said, "Yes" twice. One for the prom and the other to marry.

"Well, what are y'all waiting for?" Jamal said as he stood at the door holding out his hand to walk Tianna down the aisle.

She grabbed Jamal's hand and told him how much she loved him.

"I know you do, but you never looked at me the way you've always looked at this guy," Jamal said as he pointed to Jackson and gave him some hand dap.

"You better take care of her or else…"

Jamal didn't get to finish because Jackson assured him that he would.

Jamal walked Tianna down the aisle and gave her away. Jackson took Jamal's place and Jamal took Darren's place as Jackson's best man.

"I now pronounce you husband and wife. Jackson, you may kiss your beautiful bride," Reverend Greenwood announced.

The church cheered and "Let Me Know" played over the speakers.

"You're playing my song?"

"No, I'm playing *our* song," Jackson said as he kissed his wife, never wanting to come up for air.

Someone in the crowd yelled, "Get a hotel room." It was Tasha walking to embrace Tianna and her brother. Jackson hugged his sister and rubbed her stomach. He was going to be an uncle and his second child was on the way. He was in heaven on earth. Tyler ran to his mother and father, and Jackson picked him up and told him that he loved him.

"I love you too, Father."

Tyler reached over to give his mother a kiss. She embraced him and they looked like one happy family, finally complete.

Tianna and Jackson were married at Jamal's expense, but he didn't care. He loved her no matter what, and whatever made her happy, made him happy.

He knew that Jackson loved Tianna and would protect her. She was in good hands.

Jamal became one of the most eligible bachelors.
He had a few admirers but would take his time.

Tianna threw her bouquet and it landed right in Michelle's hands.
Malcolm X was like, 'That's right, that's right. You're next."
Tianna smiled and blew a kiss to Michelle.

The driver opened the door and Jackson lifted Tianna up and laid her down in the back of the limousine.

"You know it's on tonight, right?" He teased.

"That's why you got another one in the oven," Tianna said as she rubbed her belly.

"Oh, it's gon be plenty mo' buns in that oven. Believe me. We just getting startttted. You're having all my chillren," he stuttered playfully, pronouncing "children" as chillren. He let her know that he wanted a football team.

"You're so silly. I love you, Jackson Jeffrey Norwood!"

"I love you, too, Mrs. Jackson Jeffrey Norwood," he said as he closed the privacy window of the limousine.

Thank you for reading Tar Baby 2. I hope that you enjoyed it. Please leave a review on Amazon or Goodreads.